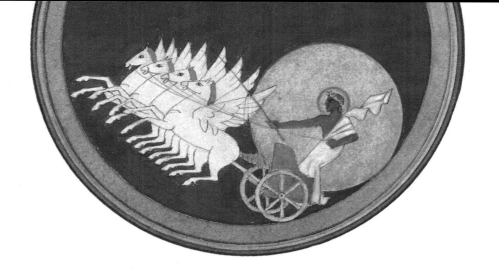

A WORLD TREASURY of

MYTHS, LEGENDS, and FOLKTALES

STORIES from SIX CONTINENTS

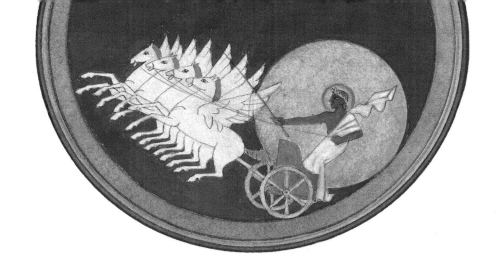

A WORLD TREASURY OF
MYTHS, LEGENDS, AND FOLKTALES

STORIES FROM SIX CONTINENTS

As told by Renata Bini

Illustrations by Mikhail Fiodorov

HARRY N. ABRAMS, INC. ✶ PUBLISHERS

CONTENTS

INTRODUCTION

THERE ARE A NUMBER of ways to look at myths, legends, and folktales. They can be religious testimonies, anthropological documents, moralistic stories, or narratives meant purely for enjoyment. Most of the stories belong to a prescientific world in which emotions prevail over rational thought. As these stories illustrate, the ancients asked many questions about the meaning of natural creations and phenomena, such as the origin of the world and the stars or the meaning of earthquakes. It is unlikely, however, that these questions were inspired by simple curiosity or an abstract desire for knowledge. At the time that most of these stories were first told, the scientific explanations taken for granted today did not exist. Therefore, any natural phenomenon such as an earthquake that could threaten the ancients' lives was a source of alarm and terror. Today, the unknown can usually be eased by some rational, scientific explanation or theory; for the ancients, anxiety about the unknown could only be eased by means of powerful symbols that spoke more to the imagination than to the mind. It is these symbols that largely make up the content of the stories in this collection. ✳ Myths, legends, and folktales also provide a way of addressing the existential questions that people have asked throughout time. The origins of life, death, and the cosmic order are the subjects of "The Shepherd and the Weaver," "Izanagi and Izanami," "Isis and Osiris," and "How People Came to Be," while "Hiawatha and the Five

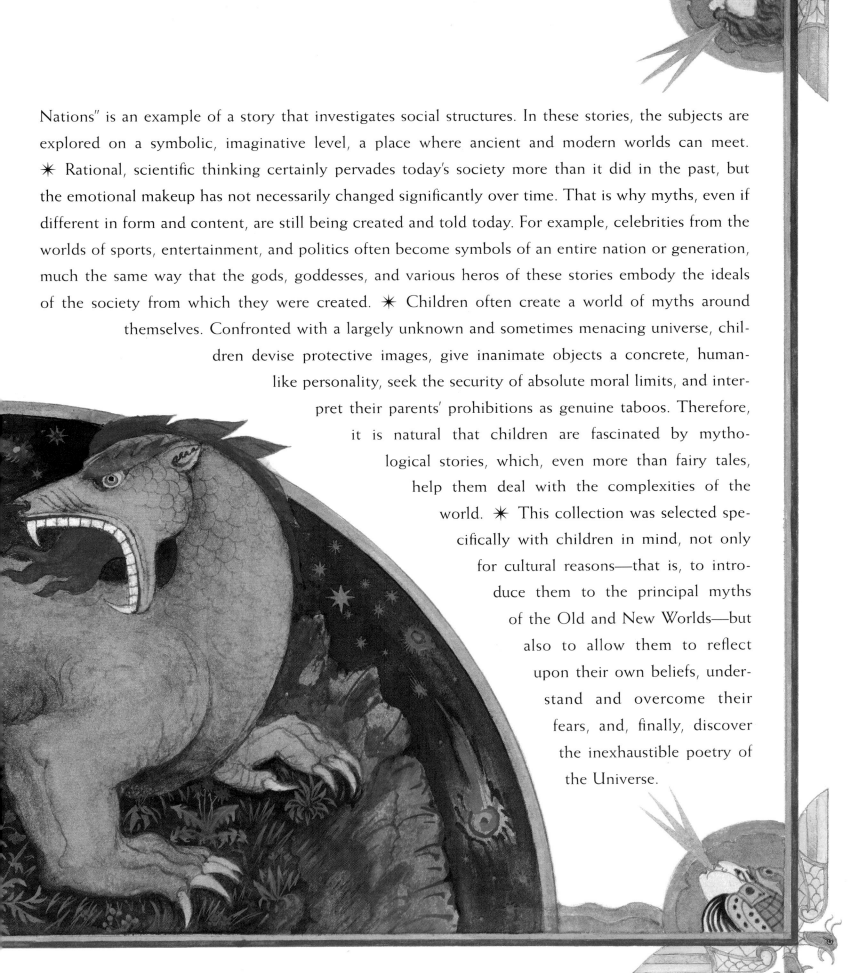

Nations" is an example of a story that investigates social structures. In these stories, the subjects are explored on a symbolic, imaginative level, a place where ancient and modern worlds can meet. ✳ Rational, scientific thinking certainly pervades today's society more than it did in the past, but the emotional makeup has not necessarily changed significantly over time. That is why myths, even if different in form and content, are still being created and told today. For example, celebrities from the worlds of sports, entertainment, and politics often become symbols of an entire nation or generation, much the same way that the gods, goddesses, and various heros of these stories embody the ideals of the society from which they were created. ✳ Children often create a world of myths around themselves. Confronted with a largely unknown and sometimes menacing universe, children devise protective images, give inanimate objects a concrete, human-like personality, seek the security of absolute moral limits, and interpret their parents' prohibitions as genuine taboos. Therefore, it is natural that children are fascinated by mytho-logical stories, which, even more than fairy tales, help them deal with the complexities of the world. ✳ This collection was selected spe-cifically with children in mind, not only for cultural reasons—that is, to intro-duce them to the principal myths of the Old and New Worlds—but also to allow them to reflect upon their own beliefs, under-stand and overcome their fears, and, finally, discover the inexhaustible poetry of the Universe.

AFRICA

THIS MAP SHOWS the six continents that have given rise to the cultures from which these stories are taken. Antarctica, the seventh continent, is not represented because it does not have a native culture.

AUSTRALIA

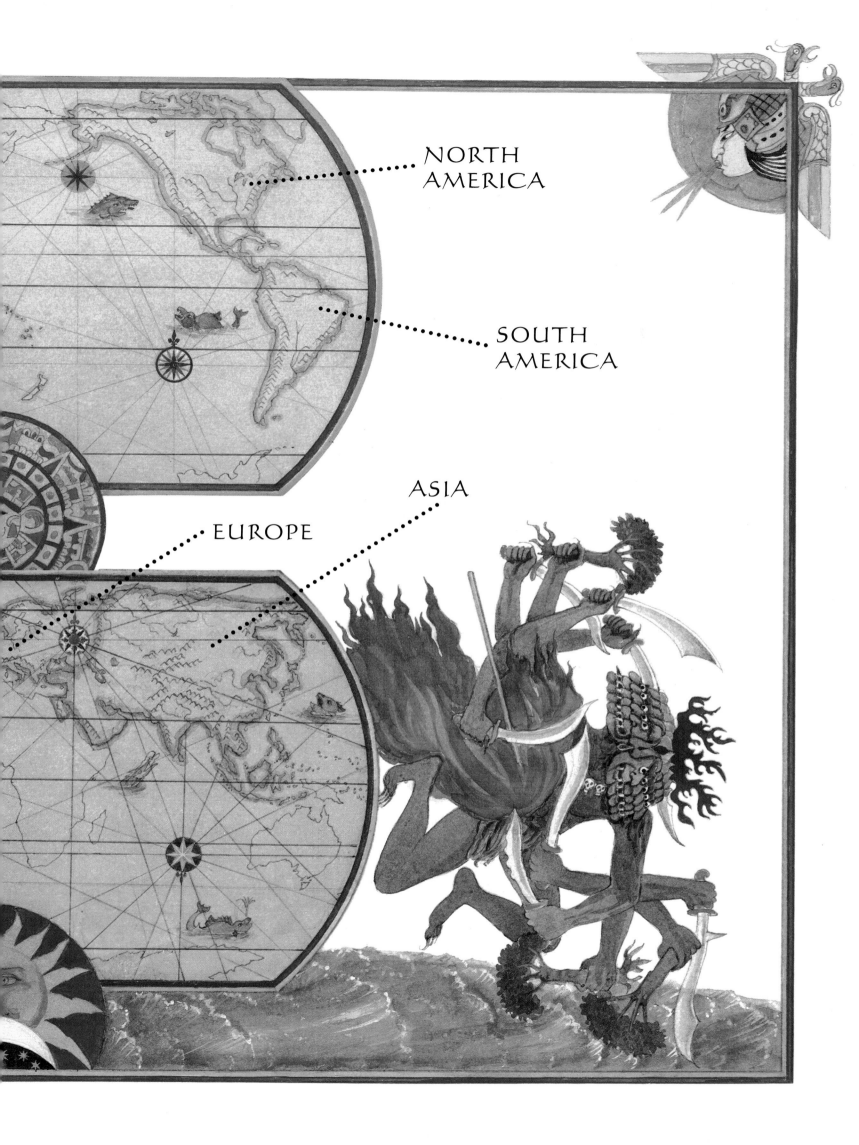

NORTH
AMERICA

SOUTH
AMERICA

ASIA

EUROPE

PELEUS AND THETIS celebrated their marriage with a lavish ceremony on Mount Ida to which they invited all the deities of Mount Olympus. They had a large reception that included Zeus, king and father of the gods and goddesses; his wife, Hera; and their children: Athena, the goddess of wisdom who was born from Zeus's head; Aphrodite, the sea-foam–born goddess of beauty and love; Hermes, the wing-footed god whose mother was Maia, not Hera; and Ares, the god of war.

Only one of the divine group was not invited—Eris, the goddess of conflict and malicious gossip. Everybody knew Eris's amazing ability to provoke quarrels and arouse negative feelings and bad moods wherever she went. Had she been invited to the wedding, the bride and groom probably would have broken up before the end of the banquet!

Eris resented being excluded and sought revenge. She went to the garden that belonged to a group of nymphs called the Hesperides. In the garden there was a wonderful tree that bore golden apples and was guarded by Ladon, a terrible dragon that wound itself around the tree's trunk. Eris knew many tricks to assist her in such situations, so she was able to sneak into the garden and steal an apple before the dragon noticed. She carved secret words into the apple and slyly made her way to Mount Ida. Hiding behind a tree, Eris awaited her chance. When all the gods and goddesses had gathered at the banquet table, she tossed the fruit toward them and ran away.

The deities were dining merrily when they noticed a golden apple drop onto the middle of the table as if from the sky. After recovering from their initial

surprise, they approached the fruit and read the message carved into it:

For the fairest

Athena, Hera, and Aphrodite looked at one another. Who of them, the three fairest goddesses of all, would claim the fruit?

"The fruit should come to me!" exclaimed Hera. "I am the fairest!"

"You? I am the fairest!" cried Athena.

"Who could be fairer than I, the goddess of love?" marveled Aphrodite.

The three goddesses argued and argued. Zeus was extremely

annoyed by the bickering, but he did not dare intervene in a situation that was too much even for him. He decided to deal with the problem by calling upon someone else to do the judging.

A young shepherd named Paris was grazing his herd on the slopes of Mount Ida. Paris was actually the prince of Troy, whose father, Priam, had abandoned him because he had had a dream that Paris would one day destroy his country. Paris was very attractive and Zeus decided he would make the perfect judge, so he sent Hermes, the divine messenger, to summon Paris to the party.

When he arrived, Paris stared at the golden fruit in his hand and shook his head. "How can I, a simple shepherd, judge divine beauty?" he said. "I will divide the apple equally among the goddesses."

"No, no," cried Hermes. "That is not possible. Great Zeus commands you to choose."

Paris sighed and begged the goddesses to accept his decision

no matter what the outcome would be. He decided to interview each goddess privately. The first was Hera. "If you choose me as the fairest," she said, "I will make you the richest of all men and allow you to rule all of Asia!"

Paris laid his hand over his heart. "You are splendid, divine Hera," he said. "But before I can choose, I must see the others. I will not be corrupted."

"If you name me the fairest," Athena said when it was her turn, "I will make you the most fascinating, wisest, and strongest of men." Paris gave the same reply he had given Hera.

Then it was Aphrodite's turn. Paris's heart sank the instant he spotted her. He was in love.

The goddess smiled. "Your eyes say that I am the fairest, but restrain yourself," she said. "How could my divine life and your mortal life meet? It is not possible. But I know of another—mortal—woman for you. Her name is Helen, and she is as fair as I."

"If there is such a woman my heart already beats for her!" Paris replied and handed the apple to Aphrodite.

The goddess instructed him to journey to the kingdom of Menelaus, where the fair Helen lived. With Aphrodite's help, Paris stole Helen away, sparking the flames that erupted into the Trojan War. His father's dream had come true, but that is another story.

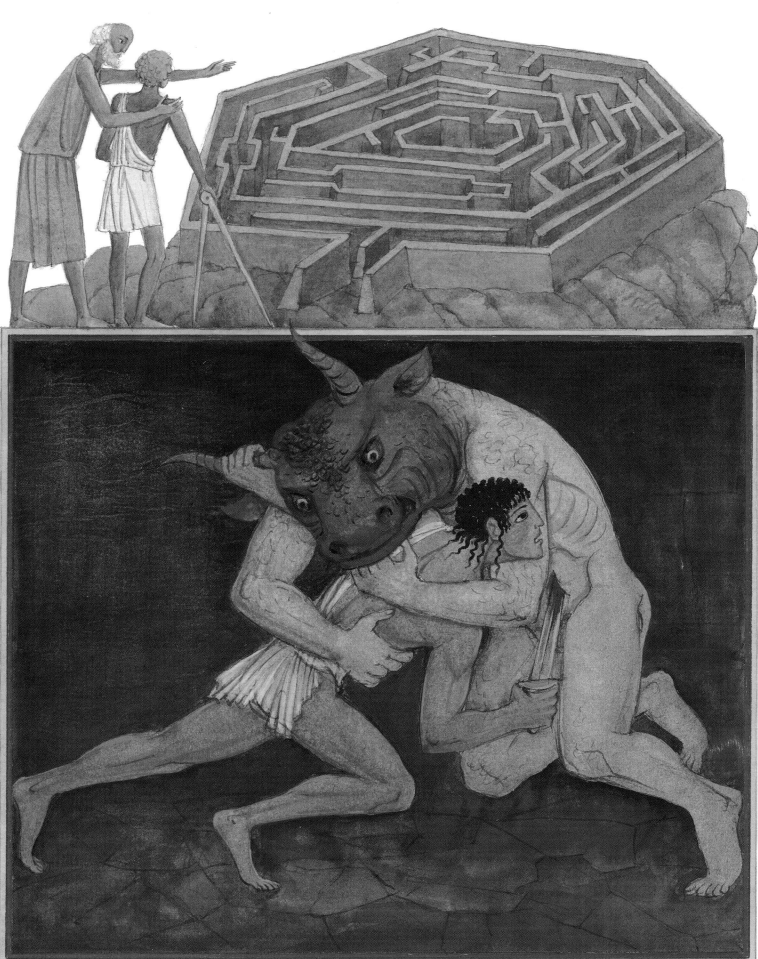

ONCE UPON A time there was a Greek architect named Daedalus whose fame had spread far beyond the borders of his homeland. One day he traveled to the island of Crete where King Minos commanded him to build a labyrinth in which the King could hide his son, the Minotaur. The Minotaur was a monstrous being who had the body of a man and the head of a bull. He lived on human flesh, and every year seven boys and seven girls were brought from Athens to be sacrificed as food for him.

With the help of his son Icarus, Daedalus built the labyrinth. Its layout was so complicated that the monster would never be able to find his way out. The labyrinth solved the problem of where to keep the Minotaur, but it did not stop the slaughtering of the children.

Three years after the labyrinth was built, a young man named Theseus arrived in Crete intending to kill the ferocious Minotaur and thus put an end to the sacrifices. Ariadne, one of Minos's daughters, came to him. "Oh, Theseus, even if you succeed in killing the Minotaur," she said, "there are thousands of rooms, hallways, and tortuous tunnels. You will never be able to find your way out!"

Theseus refused to give up. Ariadne had in the meantime fallen in love with him and wanted to do whatever she could

to help, so she asked Daedalus for advice.

"There is only one way to get out of the labyrinth alive," the architect said. "Prepare a long coil of yarn for Theseus and tell him to unroll it on his way in. He can then use the yarn to guide him when he is ready to leave."

That very night Theseus entered the labyrinth with the coil Ariadne prepared for him. As he followed its twists and turns, Theseus unrolled the ball of yarn

until he reached the heart of the maze. Soon he stood face-to-face with the Minotaur.

The monster instantly hurled himself upon the young hero. The beast was very powerful and Theseus struggled for a long time. Several times he feared he was about to die, but he eventually managed to run his sword through the Minotaur. Theseus then turned back, followed the yarn, and soon made his way out of the labyrinth. In order to flee the wrath of

Minos, he and Ariadne immediately boarded a ship and sailed away from Crete.

When Minos heard about the murder, he ordered Daedalus to the royal palace. The king was convinced that only the architect could have advised Theseus on how to escape the labyrinth.

"Let Daedalus and his son be taken to the labyrinth," Minos commanded. "The place they have built will become the place of their death!"

Daedalus and Icarus were left in one of the labyrinth's countless chambers. Even they did not know how to escape and they did not have Ariadne's yarn to guide them. Without food or water, they would surely not live long. Then Daedalus saw something that gave him an idea.

The labyrinth had no roof, so there were many bird feathers on the ground. Honeycombs sticky with wax had blown in from the outside and stuck to the walls. Daedalus gathered up the feathers and attached them to one another with the beeswax to make wings for himself and his son. As he attached a pair to Icarus he gave him a stern warning. "With these wings we will be able to fly far away from Crete and its labyrinth," he said. "But remember not to fly too high or close to the sun."

So father and son took off into the sky. They quickly flew over the labyrinth and were soon flying high above the sea. Icarus loved the feeling of flying. Seized with joy and enthusiasm, he began circling around in the air.

"Do not fly so high!" his father called out, but Icarus was not listening. Every circle took him farther and farther up. As he rose, the sun became hotter and hotter.

"Look out, Icarus!" his father shouted.

But Icarus was already flying too high to hear his warning. The sun's heat began to melt the wax and soon the wind carried away the feathers of Icarus's wings like autumn leaves. Icarus began to fall and was filled with fear. He waved his arms and yelled for his father, pleading for his help. But what could Daedalus do? The old man could only watch in horror as his son fell into the sea below and disappeared beneath the waves. And that was the death of Icarus, who did not heed his father's warning.

ERACLES WAS
the son of Zeus, the
king of the gods, and
of a mortal woman, Alcmena,
the queen of Thebes. That made
Heracles a demigod, a half man
and half god. He was therefore
blessed with extraordinary strength.
While still in his cradle he strangled with his bare hands two great
serpents that had attacked him.
At eighteen he killed a fierce lion
that had slaughtered entire herds.
He skinned the beast, and then
wore the lion skin as a symbol of
his feat.

Heracles had many adventures,
but the most famous were the
twelve labors imposed upon him
by Eurystheus, king of Tiryns.
Eurystheus had demanded these
labors as a test of Heracles's
strength and as a way of deter-
mining if Heracles was worthy of
obtaining immortality. The most

19

terrible of all these labors was most certainly the twelfth and last.

"You must go down to Tartarus, in the Underworld, and capture Cerberus, the three-headed dog who lives there," Eurystheus commanded.

Tartarus was the most dreadful part of the realm of the dead, the place where the souls of the wicked suffered every kind of torment. The gods had ordered the ferocious dog Cerberus to guard Tartarus and tear to pieces anyone who tried to escape.

Heracles left Tiryns dressed in his customary lion skin and armed with a large club, a bow, and arrows. After a long journey he arrived at a cave that led deep into the bowels of the earth where Tartarus was located. Heracles followed the passageway until he reached an underground river with dark and churning waters. The shape of a boat emerged slowly out of the misty veil that wafted over the river. The boatman was an old man who had a shaggy beard and shining eyes.

"Who dares, still living, to cross the River Acheron?" the old man exclaimed.

Heracles stepped forward swinging his club. "He who wishes to pass bears the name Heracles," he declared. "Do you oppose his will?"

Charon had heard tales of Heracles's great strength and, like so many others, feared his power, so he invited him onto his boat and took him over to the other side. When they got there, a mass of mournful figures pressed toward

them. They were the souls of the dead. Among them Heracles recognized old friends, who greeted him, and old enemies, who cursed him. Heracles was not afraid of the shadows until he noticed the soul of the horrid figure of Medusa. He immediately raised his club to defend himself.

Medusa was indeed one of the most terrible monsters that ever lived. Her eyes were flames that had the power to turn to stone anyone who met her blazing stare; instead of hair, a mass of snakes writhed about her head; and two great tusks burst forth from her mouth. Heracles was about to attack Medusa when a burst of

laughter came from behind and stopped him. It was Hades, god of the dead.

"What are you afraid of, Heracles?" he asked laughing. "The dead cannot harm the living, and Medusa has been dead a very, very long time. What you see is only her soul. Now tell me, what brings you to my desolate realm?"

Heracles explained why he had come and Hades again began to laugh. "You want Cerberus?" he asked. "Well then, if you can tame him using neither club nor arrows, the dog shall be yours." He pointed Heracles in Cerberus's direction.

The dog lived by the banks

of the River Styx. As Heracles approached, Cerberus bounded forward, all three heads howling and barking. When Heracles was only a few steps away, the monster leapt into the air bearing three sets of snapping fangs, ready to tear him to shreds. But Heracles kept calm. He reached out and grabbed Cerberus by the middle throat. The dog snarled and tried desperately to free itself, but Heracles's fingers tightened around its throat and did not let go. His arms swollen with muscles as hard as rocks, Heracles held the dog high in the air. Finally, half strangled, Cerberus surrendered.

When King Eurystheus and his court saw Heracles enter the palace with the fierce Cerberus on a leash, they were seized with terror and fled in every direction. Only Eurystheus, paralyzed with fear, stayed where he was. "Now that I have seen Cerberus, I beg you to take him back to Tartarus, and, by all the gods, may he remain there!" he pleaded.

And that was how Heracles accomplished his last labor. He proved himself worthy of becoming immortal and the gods and goddesses welcomed him to Mount Olympus, their sacred home.

THE CITY OF ALBA
Longa crowned the hills
of Latium and was the
greatest city for miles and miles
around. It was worthy of the palace of King Procas, a wise ruler
who reigned in peace for many
years. Procas had two sons,
Numitor, a soft-spoken, simple
man, and Amulius, the younger
of the two, who was greedy and
cruel. By law, the throne passed
to Numitor, the firstborn, but
Procas feared that after he died
Amulius would attempt to depose
his brother. In hopes of prevent-
ing this from happening, Procas
decided to make a deal with his
greedy son. "I will leave you the
greater part of my riches, but you
must promise me that you will
acknowledge Numitor as the
lawful king when I die," he said.

Amulius agreed, but when
Procas passed on he defied both
the law and his father's will. He
drove Numitor away to the coun-
tryside and named himself king in
his place. Amulius knew that it
was not in Numitor's nature to try
to regain the throne, but he did
fear that his brother's sons might
one day claim their right. Therefore, he ordered his servants to
kill his two nephews. As his niece,
Rhea Silvia, was a priestess of the
goddess Vesta, he locked her
away in the house of the Vestals.

Amulius knew that the priestesses were forbidden to have children, so he now felt safe.

But divine Mars, god of war and protector of the city of Alba Longa, had watched Amulius's cruelty with disgust. He sent a dream to Rhea Silvia in which she saw herself crowned with laurel in a garden, looking at two saplings that quickly grew to be majestic trees. She had the same dream for seven consecutive nights until she realized that something extraordinary was about to happen. Indeed, some months later, Rhea Silvia gave birth to twins—her sons by the god Mars.

When Amulius heard of the birth he became furious. He ordered his soldiers to take Rhea Silvia and her children to the Tiber River and drown them. Rhea Silvia disappeared into the swirling water and everyone thought she was dead. What they did not know was that Tiberinus, the god of the river, had saved her and made her immortal. In the meantime, her babies, who were placed in a basket, were carried away by the whirling currents.

IN THE REED BEDS ON the riverbank, a mother wolf was searching for food for herself and her cubs. On the river she noticed a strange object moving toward the bank as if pushed by some mysterious force. It finally washed ashore a few steps away from her. The wolf sniffed the basket warily. Driven by her hunger, she scratched it with one paw. The basket opened, and the wolf jumped back when she saw two pink newborn humans. She was about to devour them when a voice vibrated among the reeds by the river: "I am Mars, protector of wolves. I command you to care for those babies, for they were born to me and Rhea Silvia!"

The wolf bowed her head and offered the babies the food she had already gathered for herself. She then gently took them in her mouth and carried them to her lair where, for many days, she nursed them lovingly along with her own three cubs. Although Mars was pleased with the way she cared for them, he wanted his sons to know human affection too. He sent a shepherd, Faustulus, to take them home. Faustulus named them Romulus and Remus and raised them with all the love and care of a natural father.

When they had grown and learned the story of their birth, Romulus and Remus left for Alba Longa to lay claim to the throne. The people of the city had little love for Amulius and there were many who were prepared to fight against him. The twins had no trouble finding allies and eventually they gathered enough rebels to attack the palace and kill the evil usurper. When all was said and done, Romulus and Remus placed the elderly Numitor upon the throne.

After they had been in Alba Longa for some time, the twins decided to build a city on the Tiber River to honor their father, Mars. They agreed that only one of the brothers could rule the new city. Who would it be?

"Let us await a sign of the divine will," suggested Remus.

Romulus agreed and the twins separated. They each went atop

a hill to await a sign from the sky. Remus saw a flock of six vultures fly by and rejoiced. That was the sign! He was sure that he was the divinely chosen one. When he came down from the hilltop, however, he learned that Romulus had seen twelve vultures fly overhead. Remus admitted that his brother was the chosen one, but he was seized with envy.

Remus resentfully watched Romulus trace the area where the walls of the new city would rise. Overcome with jealousy, he said, "What is this? A pen for goats? My brother will rule a city of goats?"

Romulus warned his twin. "Be careful," he said. "Do not cross the sacred line. Do not mock what the divine have chosen!"

But Remus's envy was so great that he could not contain himself. He continued to chide his brother. "Look, Romulus!" he said. "Do you

see how easy it is to conquer your city?" His voice was full of disdain as he trounced around the construction area.

As hard as he tried, Romulus was unable to swallow the insult—an insult to him, Mars, and the city's future inhabitants. He drew his sword and in his rage stabbed Remus in the chest. For an instant a look of disbelief crossed his brother's face and then he fell to the ground without a sound.

Romulus stared at Remus's limp body and immediately burst into tears. What had he done?

Despite his grief, Romulus was overcome with a feeling that his city would be great. It would be a city whose inhabitants would rush to take arms against anyone who threatened it. And it was in this way that Rome, the eternal city that was the center of civilization for so many years, was born.

L OKI, THE TROUBLE-
maker, sneaked into the
house of Thor, the god
of thunder. Thor was away at the
time, and Loki, seeing Thor's wife,
Sif, asleep, decided to cut off all
her hair just for fun. As he was
finishing his horrible prank, Thor

came home. When he saw his wife
without hair he roared like thunder
and grabbed Loki by the throat.

"You rogue!" he cried. "I will
punch out all your teeth!"

Scared by Thor's threat, Loki
promised to repair the damage.
He would have his elf friends

make Sif a mane of gold that
would grow from her head as if
it were her own. The elves did
as they were told and a short
time later gave Loki the hair.
To further appease Thor, Loki
also gathered a finely chiseled
spear from the god Odin and a

handsome boat from the god Frey. The spear never missed its mark, and the boat always sailed without a mishap and could be folded up and put in a pocket.

Loki was headed to Thor's house to bestow the gifts when he noticed the twin dwarfs Brok and Sindri working in their shop. He could not resist the opportunity to boast about his treasures. "I will bet my head that as skilled as you are, you could not create anything more exquisite than these fine objects!" he exclaimed as he entered their shop.

Brok and Sindri, troubled by Loki's slur on their valued reputation as artisans, accepted the wager. Odin, Thor, and Frey would be the judges. They set to work immediately. Sindri placed the skin of a boar into their kiln and urged Brok not

to stop working the bellows that fanned the fire for even a second. Loki was confident he would win the bet but wanted to be absolutely sure. He transformed himself into a fly and stung Brok's arm to distract him. However, the dwarf did not flinch and completed his task. When Sindri took the skin out of the kiln it had become a real boar with golden bristles that shone like the sun.

Sindri then placed a block of gold into the kiln and again implored Brok not to stop pumping the bellows. Loki, still disguised as a fly, landed on Brok's neck and stung him as hard as he could. The dwarf barely shook his head. A short while later, Sindri removed a wonderful ring from the kiln that would reproduce eight rings identical to itself every nine nights.

The third time, Sindri placed a piece of iron in the kiln and urged his brother as before. Loki, the fly, who was becoming increasingly nervous, landed on one of Brok's eyelids and stung him until he bled. The dwarf dropped the bellows for a moment, waved the fly away, and returned to his task. But that one moment was enough to wreck the hammer they were making. Sindri saw what had happened and became enraged. "The piece is ruined!" he shouted.

When the hammer was taken out of the kiln, the defect was clear: the handle was too short. There was nothing more that could be done.

Loki and Brok took their gifts to the judges. Loki gave the gods the hair, the boat, and the spear, while the dwarf gave the boar to Frey, the ring to Odin, and the hammer to Thor. This last seemed like a useless gift, but Brok explained that the hammer would never miss its mark and would return to the hand of the one who threw it. It could also become small enough to be hidden under one's shirt. Despite the short handle, the gods were overjoyed. They declared the hammer the finest gift of all and the dwarf the victor of the wager.

Brok claimed Loki's head as his reward and prepared to cut it off. In desperation, Loki cried, "My head is yours, but my neck is mine! I forbid you to harm it!"

As it was impossible to cut off Loki's head without severing his neck, Brok was forced to abandon his plan. He settled for sewing Loki's mouth shut. The gods were very pleased with this. At least for a while, the rascal would be quiet!

31

BALDER, THE GOD of light, was tortured by nightmares. Even though he knew that he was loved by all for his goodness and beauty, every night he dreamed that someone was about to kill him. His father, Odin, the god of war, was worried about his son. On his eight-legged horse Odin galloped to Niflheim, the land of the dead, to the grave of Volva, the visionary who knew the secrets of the future. Odin used his powers to force her out of her grave and questioned her about the meaning of his son's nightmares.

"Beer and mead will soon be mixed for Balder," replied Volva.

Odin was horrified, for this meant his son would die! When Odin asked how Balder's death would come about, Volva answered: "Hoder, the blind god, will kill him."

Odin returned home and told Frigga, his wife, of the fate that awaited their son. Driven by fear for her son's life, Frigga left on a long voyage across the countries

of the world. She persuaded everything she met to swear never to harm her son. Air, water, earth, fire, plants, animals, and stones all swore that oath. Only the little mistletoe plant did not take the oath. Frigga assumed that it was too small and harmless to be of any danger.

So Balder became invulnerable, and the gods celebrated with a game. They hurled stones and arrows at him, stabbed him with spears, and struck him with a sword, but nothing could wound him. Only Loki, the troublemaker, did not participate in the game. He liked cruel jokes and such harmless play did not amuse him at all. Disguising himself as an old woman, he went to Frigga and tricked the goddess into disclosing that the mistletoe was the only thing that had not taken the oath.

Loki went into the forest and plucked a twig of mistletoe that grew on the trunk of an apple tree. He sharpened one end and then returned to the gathering of gods and goddesses. As before,

the deities were busy throwing things at Balder. Loki went up to Balder's brother Hoder, who was blind, and handed him the little stick of mistletoe. "Try to hit Balder with this," he said.

"How can I hit him if I cannot see him?" Holder retorted.

Loki reassured him. "Do not worry," he said. "I will guide your hand."

And so he did. Hoder threw the twig and hit his target. The mistletoe entered Balder's flesh and killed him instantly. The gods and goddesses screamed with horror and turned to accuse Loki. But the troublemaker was already gone.

As custom decreed, Balder's body was placed on a funeral pyre on his ship. But Frigga could not accept her son's death. She sent her other son, Hermod, to Hela, the queen of the dead. Hermod entreated the queen to return Balder to the world of the living.

"If all weep for Balder, the god will live again. But if even one does not, then Balder will be dead forever," Hela replied.

The gods and goddesses, the

plants, the animals, and even the stones all wept for Balder. Only Loki, who had assumed the shape of a giantess, refused to cry. There was no more hope for Balder. The enraged deities were fed up with Loki and set off to find him. The evildoer had in the meantime transformed himself into a salmon and was living in a little lake at the top of a hill. He thought he was safe in his hiding place, but the divine ones found and captured him. They took Loki to a cave and tied him tightly to three rocks. To increase his punishment, the deities placed a serpent over him so that venom dripped onto his face. But Loki was not left to suffer alone. Sigyn, his wife, was permitted to sit beside him and ease his torments.

Sigyn is still in that cave today, holding a cup in which she collects the serpent's venom. Every now and then, when the cup must be emptied, a few drops fall upon Loki's face and cause great pain. Then the god writhes in his agony, causing the earth to shake. And that shaking is what is known as an earthquake.

IME THE DWARF sat worrying in his cave. Siegfried would soon return. Mime had just managed to weld together the two broken pieces of the sword Notung, which had once belonged to Siegfried's father. However, he knew that when Siegfried came back he would break the sword across the anvil as he had so often done before. And yet, he also knew that Siegfried must have the sword if he hoped to possess the magic ring of the Nibelungen. For only with that sword could Siegfried kill Fafner, the dragon that guarded the sacred ring that provided its wearer the power to rule the world.

Siegfried appeared at the mouth of the cave with a great bear on a leash. "Come on, bear, sink your fangs into this silly dwarf who cannot create a sword worthy of me!" he said.

The dwarf showed Siegfried the sword he had welded, and, as expected, Siegfried broke it across the anvil, snapping it like a twig. "What useless thing is this?" he shouted. Mime tried

to calm him down, but Siegfried went away angrier than before.

Shortly after Siegfried left, the god Woden came to the cave disguised as a traveler. The dwarf did not know who he was and spoke to him rudely. Woden held no love for Siegfried and his family, so he did not punish the dwarf for his lack of manners. Rather, he bestowed upon Mime an important piece of advice. "The sword Notung can be repaired only by one without fear," he said. "But that one will also be the one to cut off your head!"

Woden left and Mime began shaking like a leaf. Someone without fear would kill him? Who could that be? Just then Siegfried returned, this time intending to fix the sword himself. The dwarf turned pale. Was Siegfried the one? Mime knew he had to instill the feeling of fear in Siegfried immediately. But no matter how terrifying the visions the dwarf conjured up, Siegfried was only bewildered. What was this thing called fear? He eventually stopped listening to the dwarf altogether and concentrated on the sword. He went at it diligently, and, before long, Notung was again

resplendent. Now he could take on Fafner the dragon.

In the meantime, Mime's brother Alberich paced nervously in front of Fafner's cave. The ring of the Nibelungen gave its owner the power to rule the world, and Alberich wanted that ring! Then he spotted Woden coming out of the forest and backed away in fear.

"Do not be afraid, Alberich," said the god. "I will not try to take the ring. But you must beware your brother; he is coming with a young man who means to kill Fafner. Perhaps you should make a deal with the dragon." The god then disappeared back into the forest.

Alberich called Fafner, but the dragon was asleep. There was nothing he could do. Soon after, Mime arrived with Siegfried. Mime had a plan. If the youth killed the dragon and took the ring, the dwarf could give him a deadly potion and steal the ring away and therefore prevent Siegfried from killing him.

Mime's thoughts were inter-

rupted when he saw his brother. The instant they laid eyes on one another they started to quarrel. But Siegfried blew his horn, and the two dwarfs hid in the forest. The dragon, annoyed at being awakened from his peaceful sleep, came out of the cave and approached the young man. He laughed when he laid his eyes upon him.

"Ha ha!" he scoffed. "I came out to get something to drink, and I find lunch as well!"

"It seems wrong for you to eat me," Siegfried retorted. "I think it would be better if you were the one that died."

The dragon roared and sprayed poison from his nostrils and then tried to swat Siegfried with his powerful tail. The young man leapt out of the way, drew his sword, and plunged it into the dragon's breast. Pierced in the heart, Fafner crashed to the ground. When Siegfried pulled his sword from the dragon's body, a drop of blood dripped onto his finger. Feeling a dreadful burning, the youth put his finger in his mouth and discovered that he could understand the language of birds.

"Go into the cave and fetch the ring of the Nibelungen," chirped one of the birds that flew overhead. "Take the magic helmet that lets you take any shape, too. But be careful of Mime's tricks!"

Siegfried went into the cave and successfully retrieved the ring and helmet. As he came out he was greeted by Mime who offered him a little flask. "Drink, refresh yourself, Siegfried," he said. But the dragon's blood had also given Siegfried the power to make people

tell the truth. As the dwarf gave him the flask he was forced to reveal his true intentions. "Drink and die, so I can take the ring!"

Siegfried immediately grabbed his sword and lopped off Mime's head. Alberich ran off into the forest.

"High on a crag sleeps Brunhild, Woden's daughter and the most beautiful of women," the little bird said to Siegfried. "If you can awaken her, she will be your bride. Follow me, Siegfried!"

On the way the little bird told Siegfried the story of how Brunhild had helped Siegfried's father and mother escape the wrath of Woden, who did not wish them to marry and wanted them dead. To punish Brunhild for saving them, the god infused a magic sleep upon her and set her atop a crag surrounded by flames. It was from this place that Siegfried would have to wake her.

Siegfried climbed to the top of the crag. As he reached the peak the little bird flew away. What was it afraid of? Siegfried continued on alone until he saw a traveler. It was Woden in disguise, but Siegfried of course did not know that. He caught up with the man to ask which path he should take. Woden laughed in response. "That little bird was smarter than you," he said. "It realized that I am Woden, lord of the crows and guardian of the crag!"

Woden tried to block Siegfried's path with his spear, but the young man drew his sword and sliced Woden's spear cleanly in two. Woden realized that Siegfried held the ring and was the man destined to awaken Brunhild. He collected the two pieces of his spear and left.

Siegfried climbed up to the crag, blew his horn, and in a single leap jumped over the flames. As soon as he landed on the other side, the raging fire dwindled to a mere pink cloud. Nearby a horse was sleeping in the shade of a fir tree and an armed knight was sleeping under his shield. Siegfried raised the knight's shield and slipped the helmet off to reveal a woman's face and mane of blonde curls. His heart leapt in his chest. He bent to kiss her. The woman opened her eyes and smiled at him. "I greet you, young hero, you who have roused me from my magic slumbers. What is your name?" she asked.

Siegfried placed his hand over his heart. "I am Siegfried, my beloved, I am Siegfried, forever yours!" he declared.

"As I am yours, for all eternity," murmured Brunhild. The two lovers left the crag hand in hand.

PRINCE IVAN WAS the bravest hunter in all of Russia. He never used the common travel routes but preferred the most difficult paths that penetrated into the deepest forests and forced him to climb up steep, craggy cliffs that no one else would have dared to face. One day when he was out hunting, the prince came upon a glade he had never seen before. A little waterfall gurgled out of a rock wall, and Ivan, who was thirsty, went to it immediately. Near the waterfall was a fabulous apple tree that bore golden fruit. A splendid bird with long, flame-colored feathers was roosting on one of the tree's branches.

The prince whipped out an arrow, pulled back his bow, and let it fly. The bird avoided the arrow and tried to escape, but the prince grabbed it before it could fly away. "Let me go, Prince Ivan, and I will reward you," the bird wailed in a human voice. "Here, take one of my feathers. If you are ever in danger, wave it, and I will come to your aid."

The prince was persuaded to free the bird and continued on his way with one of the bird's feathers. He soon came upon an enormous castle that was surrounded by hundreds of statues of knights. The castle's great gates opened and a band of maidens came out skipping and singing. One of them was so mesmerizing that the prince was seized with an irresistible desire to speak with her.

Ivan approached the girl but she paled in horror when she saw him. "Quickly flee this unhappy place!" she cried. "This is the home of the immortal magician Kaschei. If he sees you here he will turn you into a statue exactly

like the ones you see everywhere around you."

"I am Prince Ivan, son of the czar," the young man replied. "I fear no one! Lovely maiden, tell me your name."

The girl ran off toward the castle followed by the others. "My name is Zarevna!" she called out and then disappeared behind the enormous gate.

The prince lingered outside the castle, uncertain of what to do. When night fell, his desire to see Zarevna overcame his caution, and, without further hesitation, he pounded on the door. A gusty wind arose, and thunder and lightning split the sky. Monstrous two-headed demons were belched from the earth, causing a terrible commotion. A lightning bolt flared between the clouds and illuminated a shadowy figure—Kaschei, the magician!

The magician raised his arms and chanted as the demons advanced toward Ivan. As the chant continued, Ivan's legs became stiffer and stiffer, colder and colder. The prince was turning into a statue! In desperation he seized the firebird's feather and waved it furiously. A flaming dot appeared in the sky and rapidly approached the castle.

The dot transformed into the blazing form of the magical bird, and the demons covered their eyes and ran screaming in every direction. The ground shook,

gaped open, and in a flash swallowed up the infernal whirl. The wind dropped, and the clouds parted. A great silence fell all around. No trace remained of the demons or of Kaschei. But Ivan was sure the magician was still alive. The firebird guided him back to the apple tree with the golden fruit. "Look under the tree. Kaschei's immortal soul is there," he said.

Ivan saw a duck's egg inside a hole between the roots and realized it was Kaschei. The

prince threw the egg in the air. When it hit the ground, the egg dissolved into a cloud of smoke and flames, and a shriek echoed throughout the forest. The evil magician Kaschei was dead.

The castle walls crumbled, and the statues of knights returned to life. The maidens, free at last, embraced their sweethearts, and Zarevna ran smiling to Ivan. They held hands and swore eternal love as the firebird soared above them in the sky, melodiously singing its ancient songs.

THERE HAD BEEN no peace in Britain since the day King Uther Pendragon died. King Uther had left no heir, and the families of the nobility were constantly fighting among themselves to determine who would ascend the throne. The only one who could restore peace in Britain was the powerful enchanter Merlin, the king's councillor. But no one knew where he was.

One Christmas Eve an astonishing announcement was made: the following day, Merlin would address the knights in the great church of London. At the appointed hour, the church filled with men at arms. Everyone was trying to guess what the sorcerer would say. Suddenly there was a great silence, and a shiver went through the hall. A tall, thin, old man with a long, white beard, dressed in the long tunic of the Druids appeared on the steps of the altar. Merlin!

"Noble knights," he said. "For some time you have been crossing your swords in order to give Britain a king. Now I say this to you: one sword will decide the new sovereign!"

Merlin went into the sacristy and disappeared. The knights had already begun to argue over the meaning of his words when they were interrupted by a guard who rushed into the church. "Come outside," he shouted. "There is something in the courtyard!"

The knights ran to look. On the old sacrificial stone was an anvil with a sword thrust through it and into the marble beneath. The stone bore a legend: "Whosoever draws this sword shall be king of Britain."

The knights elbowed one another aside in their eagerness to be the first to try; each one was certain that the throne was his by right. They pulled, they yanked, they dug their heels in, and they contracted their muscles to the point of spasm. The sword remained solidly in place. None of the knights had passed the test. Who, then, would be king? They decided that each of the area's noblemen would take part in a great tournament that would be held on New Year's Day. The winner would be named king of Britain.

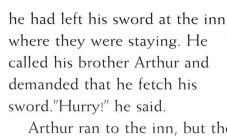

Among the various noblemen who came to London for the tournament was Sir Ector and his two sons, bold Sir Kay and young Arthur. The tournament began amid flapping pennants and fanfare. The armored knights galloped toward each other with their lances leveled. They fought with sword and shield and whacked one another with iron maces.

Sir Kay paced in anticipation of his turn. He suddenly realized he had left his sword at the inn where they were staying. He called his brother Arthur and demanded that he fetch his sword. "Hurry!" he said.

Arthur ran to the inn, but the sword was not there. He was already dreading his brother's scolding when he noticed a sword wedged into a stone in the abandoned courtyard. "Better than nothing," he thought. He withdrew it easily from the stone and took it to Sir Kay without

recognizing which sword it actually was.

When Sir Kay saw Arthur he realized that his brother had pulled the sword that so many before him could not. He knew that his brother did not know what he had done and took immediate advantage of the situation. "Look!" he shouted. "I pulled out the magic sword. I am king!"

The news spread through the camp like wildfire. Sir Ector, however, had his doubts about his often not truthful son and demanded that the test be repeated. The knights met in the courtyard of the church. Sir Ector replaced the sword and asked his son to draw it. Sir Kay tried his hardest; he pulled and pulled until his muscles looked as if they were about to burst through his armor. But the sword remained fixed in place. Sir Kay was forced to tell the truth that Arthur had brought the sword to him.

Everyone present was shocked, but they were eager to find their king. "Have the boy try!" they roared.

Arthur made his way forward. He reached his slender hand toward the hilt and grabbed it. Effortlessly, he drew the sword from the anvil and marble. Cries of exultation rang out, and flags and hats were thrown into the air. "Hurray!" everyone shouted. "Britain has found its king!"

GEB, THE GOD OF the earth, and Nut, the goddess of the sky, loved each other so much that they were never apart. In fact, they were so close that there was no room for anything to be born between them! Their father, Shu, therefore decided to separate them. With one foot he held Geb down and with the other he raised Nut up. Into the new space created between them, Nut was able to give birth to two sets of twins: two boys, Osiris and Seth, and two girls, Isis and Nephthys. Osiris married Isis, and Seth married Nephthys. But Nephthys secretly loved Osiris. Seth knew this and began to hate his brother.

Osiris and Isis became king

and queen of Egypt, and together they governed wisely, teaching their people the ways to honor the gods, the art of building temples, and the cultivation of grain. Seth saw how beloved the two rulers were, and this only fed his resentment. He decided to plot his revenge.

One day at a feast, Seth showed the guests a wonderful coffin made of rare wood and created with great skill. He said, in fake jest, for this was part of his revenge, "Do you see this marvelous piece? I will give it to whoever can fit in it and touch each of the panels with their body."

Many tried to fit in the coffin.

Some found it too small, while others found it too large. When it was Osiris's turn he laughed, eager to partake in the game. "Remember you promised, Seth!" he said to his brother. "If I fit in the coffin perfectly, you will have to give it to me."

"Do not worry, Osiris," Seth replied with an evil grin. "If that happens, you will never be without it."

Osiris lay down in the coffin, which proved to be exactly his size (of course his brother had had it made so). But when the king of Egypt tried to get out, Seth's accomplices ran up and pushed him back inside. They closed the lid, nailed it down,

and sealed it with boiling water to swell the wood. Then they took the coffin and threw it into the Nile River.

Shut up inside, poor Osiris suffocated to death. Isis cried in despair when she heard the terrible news. Dressed in traditional mourning clothes, she resolved to find her husband's coffin and went searching for it along the course of the Nile. She stopped in every village, but no one had seen it. Finally, in the land of Byblos, in Phoenicia, Isis found what she was seeking. She had Osiris's coffin loaded onto a ship, returned with it to Egypt, and hid it in a secret marsh.

One day when he was out hunting, Seth walked into the marsh and discovered his brother's coffin. Enraged, he removed the lid, tore Osiris's body into pieces, and scattered them throughout Egypt. Isis wept for a long time when she discovered what had happened to her husband's body. She boarded a boat with her sister, Nephthys, and went to search for the pieces. When she found them, Isis called Anubis, the jackal-headed god of the dead, to put Osiris's body back together.

Anubis did as he was asked and Osiris's body was put back together. Isis felt she could not live without him any longer and decided to use all her greatest powers and magic to bring him back. She and Nephthys transformed themselves into hawks and flapped their wings over Osiris's corpse for a long time. Eventually Osiris opened his eyes and sat up.

"My love!" exclaimed Isis as her husband finally regained his normal appearance.

"My love!" exclaimed the resurrected Osiris.

Husband and wife embraced once more. Isis's magic could not keep Osiris alive for more than one night. That evening, they conceived Horus, the son who would one day avenge his great father for Seth's evil actions and would govern the world with his parents' wisdom.

Although Osiris's body died again after that night, his spirit went to the realm of the After-life and became its monarch. From that place Osiris still judges the souls of the dead, rewarding or punishing according to the merits of each.

RAVANA, THE many-headed, many-armed demon, was committing every kind of evil imaginable. Earlier, Ravana had forced the god Brahma to promise that no god or demon could harm him. He had therefore become indestructible and took advantage of this privilege to do as he pleased.

"No demon or god can kill Ravana," said Vishnu, "but a man could."

Vishnu was right but he also knew that it would be difficult to find a man brave and strong enough to face Ravana. So the god came down to earth and incarnated himself as a man. Vishnu had changed form other times before: as a fish, a tortoise, a boar, a lion-man, and even a dwarf. This time he was born a baby, the son of Dasa-ratha, king of Ayodhya. He was named Rama and lived at court until he was old enough to marry.

In the land of the Vidahya, King Janaka had a very beautiful daughter named Sita. When Rama learned this, he went to Janaka to ask for her hand.

"Noble Rama," said the king. "I would be happy to consent to this marriage, but there are many suitors. I have therefore decided that only the one who can draw the bow that the god Shiva has given me can become Sita's husband."

Rama was brought into the great hall to undergo the test.

The princes who had already failed shook their heads. "No one could draw that bow," they muttered. "Even the strongest man could not draw it more than the length of a fingernail!"

Rama asked for the bow and smiled. He effortlessly drew it back as everyone around him gazed in astonishment. The bow bent farther and farther, squeaking in every fiber until, all at once, in the stunned silence of the hall, a crack echoed through the chamber. The bow was broken in two!

King Janaka summoned Sita, placed her hand in the prince's, and celebrated the marriage. Rama tenderly embraced his bride. Thus Vishnu became a man and won his first battle, but his moment to face Ravana was still to come.

A FEW YEARS AFTER Rama and Sita's marriage, a court intrigue forced Rama to leave his father-in-law's realm. He was exiled to the forest with his beautiful bride and his brother Lakshmana.

In the meantime, the demon Ravana was plotting to abduct Sita and make her his wife. To carry out his plan, he sent an enchanted deer into the clearing where Sita liked to rest. When she saw the splendid creature, she was entranced by its beauty and filled with an irresistible impulse to caress it. But as she moved toward it, the deer slipped swiftly into the forest and then disappeared among the trees. Overwhelmed by the desire to possess the deer, Sita called to her husband to help her catch it. Rama went after it with Lakshmana, but not before tracing a circle around his wife and insisting she stay inside of it in order to protect her from demons.

As soon as the men left, Sita heard a tremulous voice. "A little food, for pity's sake. A little food for an old priest of Brahma."

Sita turned to see a very old man in a filthy saffron-colored sari

holding a wooden bowl. "I beg you, lady, give me a little food," the priest said again.

"Very willingly," replied Sita. "As soon as my husband returns, we will go to our cottage where you may have some food and rest."

"Good lady," the old man said. "I am too weak to walk. I have not eaten for three days, and . . . "The old man fainted without finishing the sentence.

Overcome with empathy, Sita ran to help him without thinking that she was leaving the magic circle. Immediately the old

Brahmin—who was actually Ravana—tore off his disguise and threw himself upon her, squeezing her tightly in his many strong arms. He forced her onto his flying cart, which was drawn by golden-headed mules, and headed for the island of Lanka. Sita wept and called for help, but only the forest and the river below her could hear.

Ravana's palace was an impenetrable fortress with very high walls that was guarded by a demon army. Ravana was sure that Sita would never be able to escape

and that no one would be able to come to her aid. He was therefore prepared to wait patiently until Sita agreed to become his wife.

When Rama and Lakshmana found Sita missing, they began to look for her.

"On the island of Lanka, your wife weeps for her sorrowful destiny," the forest leaves whispered.

"In Ravana's castle, your wife weeps as she waits for her husband," the river's waves murmured.

Rama and Lakshmana heard these cries, but how could they believe what the leaves or the river had to say? They ignored the pleas and continued to search in vain.

One day Rama and Lakshama came upon a dying man who had been seriously wounded while fighting Ravana at his castle. As the man closed his eyes for the final time, he, too, revealed the place where Sita was being held prisoner. Although they were excited, Rama and Lakshmana discussed the matter cautiously. Without a powerful ally they would never be able to defeat Ravana alone. Accordingly, they went to see Sugriva, the lady of the monkeys, who had been disowned by one of her half-brothers. Rama helped Sugriva regain her realm, and, in return, she placed a mighty army of

monkeys at his disposal and ordered Hanuman, son of the wind, to lead them on their journey.

The men traveled to Rama's castle. When they reached the seashore, Hanuman crossed the waves in a single leap and joined Sita, who was still held prisoner in the palace. It was not up to him to free her, but Hanuman let Sita know that Rama was on the way. The monkeys built a bridge over the sea, and soon Hanuman's army attacked the fortress.

A bloody battle was set in motion and thousands of demons and monkeys died. In the end, the fortress fell and the demons fled, leaving the evil Ravana to

face Rama alone. Rama hurled himself against Ravana in a gruesome fight, but every head of Ravana's that Rama succeeded in cutting off grew back instantly. He realized his sword was useless against the demon, so he seized the gods' magic spear and threw that at him instead. The spear went through Ravana's chest and killed him instantly. Sita was finally free!

Husband and wife returned home. Rama was crowned king and lived happily ever after with his beautiful wife.

A POOR SHEPHERD lived alone. His only possessions were a tiny piece of land and an old ox that was actually a good genie. One day the ox noticed that his master was particularly melancholy. "Do not be sad or lonely, Shepherd," he said. "If you follow my advice, I will help you find a wife."

The Shepherd listened to the ox's instructions and the following morning went to a spot where the river formed a peaceful pool. Hidden in the bushes, the astonished young man watched seven beautiful maidens bathing among the water lilies. They laughed and squealed happily, entirely unaware that they were being watched. They were the celestial maidens that had come down to earth to bathe and refresh themselves.

As the ox had instructed him, the young man cautiously crawled to where the maidens' robes lay forgotten on the riverbank and stole one, then ran to hide it behind his house. When he returned to the river, he saw

that each of the celestial maidens had returned to heaven except for one. As soon as she saw the Shepherd, the girl reproached him. "I am the Weaver, daughter of the August of Jade, Emperor of the Sky," she said. "Quickly, give me back my robe. I cannot go home without it."

"Never!" refused the Shepherd. "You will be my wife."

The Weaver thought about it a little, then accepted. And so the two were joined in marriage, and after a few years a son and a daughter were born. One day the Weaver said to her husband, "Dear, now that we have been married for some time, you could give me my robe back."

The Shepherd assumed there was no longer any reason to keep the robe hidden, so he gave it back to his wife. No sooner had the Weaver put it on than she flew off and disappeared quickly into the sky, leaving her husband agape.

"Never fear," said the ox. "Hang two baskets on a pole and place the children in them. Then take the basket on your shoulders and grab my tail."

The Shepherd did as he was told, and in no time the ox was headed toward the sky, pulling the Shepherd and his children behind him. As soon as he arrived in Heaven, the Shepherd went to the marvelous palace of the August of Jade.

He entered a great hall. The floor was made of soft clouds, and the ceiling held an immense vault of rainbows supported by jade pillars. The August of Jade was seated on a throne of gold and silver. "Young man, what destiny has guided you to the stars' eternal places?" he asked the Shepherd.

The Shepherd related his misfortunes and entreated the Emperor to give him back his wife. The Emperor summoned his daughter and asked for her version of the story.

"Great Father," the Weaver explained. "I love my husband and my children, but I am a celestial creature and could no longer live on earth. That is why I ran away."

The Emperor thought about what each had said and then offered a solution. "Because this man married my daughter, a divine maiden, I grant him immortality," he said. "The

Shepherd will live beside his wife forever in the sky."

The two began to rejoice, but the August of Jade continued. "You must also be punished for your trickery," he said. "Thus, I will place between you a heavenly river of stars, the Milky Way, which will divide you forever."

The Shepherd and the Weaver cried at the August of Jade's decision and sadly went to take the places he had assigned them.

The gods, however, took pity on the two lovers and asked the Emperor to lighten their sentence. He granted that once a year, on the seventh day of the seventh month, husband and wife could meet.

To this day, whoever looks up at the sky may see the two lovers. On one side of the Milky Way sits the constellation of the Weaver, which Westerners call Aquila, the Eagle, and on the other sits the Shepherd, also called Lyra, the Lyre. On the seventh day of the seventh month when the two are allowed to meet, all the magpies rise into the sky with twigs in their beaks and weave a great bridge across the Milky Way. The Shepherd embraces the Weaver who weeps from happiness, and her tears fall to earth as rain. When lovers who are far away from their beloveds feel sad, all they have to do to be comforted is to look in the sky for the Shepherd and the Weaver.

IZANAGI AND IZANAMI were asked to create the country Japan. The two gods stepped onto a floating bridge and with a long pole stirred the ocean until an island condensed from the whirlpool. Then Izanagi and Izanami joined in marriage and had many children. Izanami gave birth to the islands of Japan and to the deities of sea and earth, wind and rain. The last child was the god of fire, and Izanami, unable to bear his burning heat, perished during childbirth.

After mourning the loss of his wife for a long time, Izanagi left for the Land of Darkness where the dead live. He arrived at the door of the palace of the spirits and called for his wife loudly. "Come back, my love," he said. "We have not yet finished building the world!"

From the other side of the door Izanami called back. "I have already eaten the food of the darkness. I think it is too late for me to come back, but I will ask the spirits of this land to let me return with you," she said. "I warn you, though, do not look at me!"

Izanagi waited in front of the great door while his wife went to ask for permission to leave. A long time passed, and, tired of waiting, he entered the palace of the dead. Inside it was very dark, and Izanagi could not see anything. He broke a tooth off the comb that he always carried with him and lit it like a torch.

He focused his eyes and saw that Izanami was only a few steps away from him. Ignoring her warning, Izanagi looked at her directly. She was unrecognizable. Her beautiful hair was sparse and shaggy, her face was pale and waxen, and her body was so scrawny that her robe draped

over her like a rag. Izanagi backed away. How could this be his wife? Where was the woman he had loved so much?

Izanagi could not help himself. He turned to run. Izanami had warned him not to look at her and was angry at how horrified he looked. She therefore commanded

the spirits of the darkness to kill him. Izanami and the spirits chased Izanagi, determined to tear him to pieces. They were about to catch him when Izanami took off his hat and threw it on the ground. A vine laden with bunches of succulent grapes sprouted in the place where it fell. The spirits had until now eaten nothing but dirt and could not resist the delicious grapes, so they stopped to eat them. This gave Izanagi enough time to get away—for the moment.

When they finished the grapes the spirits returned to the chase. They were about to catch the god when he threw his comb over his shoulder. Upon touching the ground, the comb turned

into a bamboo thicket full of shoots. The shoots were deliciously tender, and the spirits stopped to eat them, again allowing Izanagi to get away.

As he emerged from the cave that led to the realm of the dead, he noticed that his wife, who had not stayed to eat with the other spirits, was only steps behind him. Izanagi took a heavy rock that lay nearby and rolled it in front of the entrance. The boulder was so big that not even a thousand men could have moved it. It would forever separate the world of the dead from the world of the living.

Izanami was enraged. "To avenge myself I will kill one thousand people every day and bring

them to the Land of Darkness!" she shouted.

"And I," replied her husband, "will have fifteen hundred babies born every day!"

And so it was that Izanami became the goddess of death, and Izanagi the god of life. On his way home, Izanagi passed through an orange grove where a clear stream ran. Dirty with the grime from the land of the dead, the god stopped to wash his face and dried it with a corner of his robe. The moment he dabbed his left eye, Amaterasu, the goddess of the sun, was born. As he dried his right eye, Tsuki-Yomi, the god of the moon, was born. Finally, he dried his nose and Susanowo, the god of thunder and storms, was born. In this way Izanagi presided over the world of the living and ensured the creation of life.

YOUNG KINTU arrived in Uganda with only a cow. As he had nothing else to eat, he lived solely on her milk. Nambi, the daughter of Gulu, the god of the Sky, fell in love with Kintu and wanted him to be her husband, but her brothers were wary of him. "Anyone who lives only on milk is no human being," they said. "How can he marry you?"

Nambi and her brothers went to their father to ask his advice. "Let us take away his cow," the god said. "If he can only live on that cow's milk then he cannot survive without the beast. If he dies, it means he is not human."

could he eat all that food? A great hole in the floor of the house offered him a wonderful solution. Kintu swiftly threw all of the food into it. Nambi's brothers came to see how he had fared. Seeing the food gone, they immediately went back to tell Gulu that Kintu had managed to eat everything. But the god of the Sky was still unconvinced.

He gave Kintu an axe. "Go split some rock to light a fire; firewood is not good enough for me."

Kintu was sure the axe would break on rock and felt there was nothing he could do. But when

he reached the mountain he saw that there were many rocks there that had already been split. He gathered them up and took them to Gulu. Gulu was impressed by what he saw but was still unsure that Kintu would be a husband worthy of his divine daughter.

He handed Kintu a vase. "Fill this vase with water," he commanded. "But the water must be only dew."

Kintu took the vase and gloomily went into the fields. How could he fill a vase with dew? He thought about it all night long. At dawn

Kintu did not die. He proved that he was human by eating leaves and roots. Gulu was still unconvinced that the man was worthy of his daughter's hand, so he devised another test. He sent Nambi to earth to fetch him. "I know where your cow is. Come with me if you want her back," Nambi said to Kintu.

Kintu went up to the Sky and was brought into a house where a meal for one hundred people had been prepared.

"You must eat everything," Gulu told him. "Otherwise you will have neither your cow nor my daughter!"

Kintu was beside himself. How

every blade of grass was heavy with dew. And his vase was filled to the brim! Kintu proudly returned the vase to Gulu.

Gulu was finally convinced that Kintu deserved to marry Nambi, but he wished to persuade the people of the Sky as well. He called his people together. "Kintu is a great man, and he may marry my daughter, Nambi. But first he must find his cow, which is now mixed in with the rest of mine," he announced.

Kintu knew very well that the king of the Sky owned thousands and thousands of cows that each looked exactly like his, and that finding his cow would be impossible. He was about to give up hope when a bee landed on his shoulder. "Do not be afraid, Kintu," the bee buzzed. "I can identify your cow. I will go with you to the pasture where all the cows are grazing and land on your cow's back. That way you will know which cow is yours."

The next morning Kintu was taken to a pasture of a thousand cows. He looked around and saw the bee resting peacefully on the branch of a nearby tree. Kintu pretended to look for his cow among the others and then proclaimed, "My cow is not here!"

Gulu's servants brought in a second herd ten times more numerous than the first. The bee remained on the tree branch. "No, my cow is not here either," Kintu said after a short while.

A third herd ten times as numerous as the second was brought to him. This time the bee flew away from the tree and Kintu followed her amid a forest of horns. Finally the bee landed on the back of a large cow.

"Here," exclaimed Kintu. "This is my cow!"

Then he saw that the bee had gone and landed on a little calf. "And this is my cow's calf that was born during the last few days," Kintu proclaimed.

The bee buzzed on to another calf, and then another. Kintu recognized each of these as his cow's calves. Gulu was thrilled. "You are indeed Kintu the great, and I give you my blessing to take my daughter into your home to be your wife," he said.

Kintu and Nambi returned to Earth along with a goat, a sheep, a hen, seeds for all plants, and, of course, the cow and all her calves. Kintu was Uganda's first and greatest king, and he ruled wisely with his wife for many happy years.

GOD HAD created the whole world with mountains, lakes, forests, savannas, deserts, animals, and plants, but human beings were still missing. God went into the savanna and dug two holes in the ground. After a few seconds, a man came out of the first hole, and a woman out of the second. They were the first man and woman to ever exist, and they knew absolutely nothing at all.

"What should we do?" they asked God.

"You must hoe the soil and plant seeds in it. Then you must build yourselves a hut where you can sleep," the Creator replied.

"And what will we eat?" the two asked.

"The seeds will eventually grow into corn, which you will cook. That will be your food," said God.

The man and woman hoed the soil and planted the seeds but not without resting many times. "It is so hard to hoe the soil! Oh, it is such hard work!" they grumbled.

Nevertheless the seeds were eventually planted and quickly grew into corn. The man and the woman were hungry, but they were too lazy to light a fire and

cook the corn, so they ate it raw. When they were tired they debated whether or not it was worthwhile to build a hut. "There is no reason to build a hut," they decided. "There are many trees in the forest and we can easily sleep on a branch without having to work so hard."

God became furious when he saw them calmly sleeping in a tree. God summoned a male monkey and a female monkey and gave them the same instructions the human beings had received. The monkeys went to work right away. They planted the seeds and built a nice hut. They lit a fire, ground the ears

of corn, and cooked them until they had delicious-smelling loaves. When they finished, they went to their hut to rest.

God felt greatly satisfied and summoned the two monkeys, took off their tails, and said, "You will be human beings."

God then summoned the man and the woman and attached the monkeys' tails to the base of their spines. "From now on, you will be monkeys," God said.

Ever since that time, the monkeys that became human beings have lived in houses, while the real first people still sleep in the trees.

THE DIVINE MANTIS was strolling in the forest when her curiosity was aroused by a sound that came from behind a bush. When she looked she saw the Ostrich plucking red berries with his beak.

"What are you doing?" the Mantis asked.

"Can't you see?" the Ostrich retorted rudely. "I am eating berries. Now leave me alone."

The Mantis noticed that the Ostrich held one of his wings tight against his side and did not raise it. A strange red glow shone from beneath.

"What is that?" the Mantis wondered to herself. "And why is the Ostrich being so careful to hide it? I must get to the bottom of this!" She decided to trick the Ostrich in order to see what he was hiding. "Those berries must be good," she said out loud. "Would you get me one, friend Ostrich?"

"Get it yourself. I am busy," the Ostrich muttered with his mouth full.

"Do me this favor, my friend," the Mantis insisted. "The best berries are the ones at the top of the bush and I cannot reach them because I am too short. But your neck is long and you can reach them easily."

This flattered the Ostrich, who was very vain. "I can do everything with my neck. I can pick even the highest berries!" he boasted.

The Ostrich got up on tiptoe and stretched as high as he could to reach the top branches. But in order to keep his balance he had to spread his wings and the object he had hidden fell to the ground. It was the burning ball of fire! The Mantis had heard that someone had stolen it. She immediately snatched it up and ran away, but the Ostrich followed close behind.

The Ostrich chased the Mantis and closed in on her quickly. Feeling trapped, the Mantis threw the ball into a termites' nest. "Run, dear Fire, or the Ostrich will keep you hidden forever beneath his wing," she said.

The Fire jumped from the termites' nest up into a tree and hid inside. The Ostrich looked and looked for it the rest of his life, but he never found the Fire again. The Fire remained in the tree. In the evenings the people of the savanna, who know the Fire's secret, break off twigs from a tree and rub them together. With the secret, they create the fires that light their villages during the clear African nights.

ONCE THERE WAS only the darkness. The darkness and Crow, who was small and weak. Crow knew that it was not a good thing to stay in the dark and silence doing nothing. Because he was too young to fly, Crow decided to hop around in the hopes that it would get him somewhere. Every time he landed, mountains, forests, rivers, and streams were formed. Crow was astonished as he saw these wonders, because he did not understand that it was he who was creating them.

Crow kept jumping farther and farther, and before he realized what was happening, he reached the end of the sky and landed on the edge of a dreadful abyss. Afraid he would fall in, he instinctively spread his wings and realized that they had become big and strong enough to carry him. In that moment, he understood that he was Tulugaukuk, the Father Crow.

He flew down into the bottom of the abyss, which was dark and empty. In the abyss, Crow created

the same things he had created by jumping up and down in the world above. He called the world down below Earth, and the world above Sky. Then Crow took a shining stone and threw it into the Sky. The stone became Sun and illuminated everything.

One day when Crow was flying around admiring his creations, he saw a great pea plant with enormous pods that was taller than a tree. Crow stopped, surprised. A pod opened abruptly, and a man stepped out! Crow had never seen such a creature and jumped back in shock. The man had never seen a crow and was equally frightened. When he got over his surprise, Crow asked the man if he was hungry.

The man *was* very hungry, so Crow showed him a shrub. "Eat the berries on that shrub," he said.

The man ate all the berries, but when he was finished he was hungrier than before. Crow took some clay and shaped a musk-ox and a caribou, which instantly galloped across the prairie. He gave the man a bow and arrows to hunt with. "Do not kill too many animals," he said, "or they will become few and you will be hungry again."

The man respected the animals that Crow created and only killed those he needed. Many years passed. Men became greedy and killed more animals, more than they needed. Eventually the respect between man and animal was lost. Crow watched until he became so angry he could watch no more. He flew up to the prairies in the sky and never came back down to Earth. Crow will only return when human beings are once again friends to the musk oxen and caribou.

GLUSKAP AND THE DRAGON AT THE SPRING

A LONG TIME AGO, Gluskap created a village where everyone lived happily. Gluskap was a spirit, a witch doctor, who could do whatever he wanted. He never grew old and is still alive today somewhere in the world. One day, the village's spring stopped giving water and a stinking slime poured out instead. It was the village's only source of water, so the chiefs decided to send an explorer to find out what had happened.

The explorer walked for a long time and finally arrived at a village inhabited by creatures that were like human beings, except they

had webbed hands and feet and snouts like frogs. Nearby ran a stream of dirty water. The explorer, who was very thirsty, asked the frog-people if he could drink some of that water even though it was dirty.

"We cannot give you anything to drink without our chief's permission," they replied. "If you follow the stream back from where you came, you will find him by the spring where the stream ends."

When the explorer reached the spring he was terrified. The chief was an enormous dragon with a belly the size of an entire valley. His mouth was as wide as a cave and stretched from ear to ear. His body was covered with bumps as big as mountains.

The dragon's feet rested in a huge puddle where the valley's water had pooled. His feet were making the water filthy! The explorer asked the dragon to give the water back to the village and explained that without it the people would die of thirst. But the dragon only laughed. "What do I care if the people die of thirst? I want all the water for myself! I want it all! All of it! All of it!" he retorted. Before the explorer could say another word, the dragon added, "I have eaten a thousand people, and now I will eat you, too."

The horrified explorer fled so fast that his heels hit the nape of his neck.

When he reached the village he told the people everything that

had happened and they began to cry. Gluskap heard the cries from the village and knew he must intervene. He colored his body with war paint, made himself as tall as a tree, and put one hundred black eagle feathers and one hundred white eagle feathers on his head. He shouted his war cry and all the earth shook. He approached a mountain and with a blow of his hand split it in two. From its core he took a great piece of very sharp flint to use as a dagger. Armed and ready, Gluskap made his way toward the dragon's spring.

Every step shook the valleys and was heard across the world. The village's inhabitants realized that great Gluskap was coming to help them.

"My people need clean water," Gluskap said when he finally reached the dragon.

"What do I care about your people?" the dragon replied. "I want all the water for myself!"

"You are ugly and your brain is full of mud. Now we will see who the water belongs to," Gluskap exclaimed.

A memorable battle ensued. Whole forests were leveled, mountains were brought down to the ground, and flames and smoke leapt up from the swamps. The dragon tried to swallow Gluskap, but the hero made himself so big that even the dragon's huge mouth could not bite him. Finally, Gluskap thrust his flint knife into the dragon's

swollen belly. Out of the wound bubbled a river of rushing water that flowed in the direction of the village.

"This is just the water my people need!" exclaimed Gluskap. He made his hand grow extremely large and squeezed the dragon until he shrank smaller and smaller. When

the dragon was the size of a frog, Gluskap threw him into the swamp.

Ever since, the dragon has lived in the swamp and his skin has remained wrinkled from Gluskap's squeezing. Gluskap returned home, and the people in the village had cool, clear water to drink for ever after.

AFTER HE DEFEATED the dragon of the spring; the Kewawkqu giants; the Medecolin witch doctors; Pamola, the terrible spirit of the night; and many other demons and spirits, Gluskap was very pleased with himself and began boasting to a woman.

"I am truly invincible," he said. "No one can defeat me!"

"Really?" the woman replied. "I think I know someone you cannot beat."

Surprised, Gluskap asked to know the name of so powerful a being.

"His name is Wasis," said the woman. "I warn you for your own sake. Stay away from him."

But Gluskap wanted to fight Wasis; only then could he prove he was the most powerful being in the world. So the woman took him to her village, led him into a tepee, and pointed to a baby sitting on the floor sucking a piece of maple sugar.

"There," said the woman. "That is Wasis. He is little, but powerful. Do not provoke him."

"We shall see," answered Gluskap. He swelled his chest and shouted, "I am Gluskap! Come fight me!"

Wasis paid no attention to him and continued to peacefully suck on his piece of sugar.

"Did you hear me? Come fight!" Gluskap said again. The baby seemed utterly unconcerned, so the hero uttered his terrible war cry to scare him.

Little Wasis looked at him for a moment, then opened his mouth. "Waaahh! Waaahh!" he wailed. It was now his turn to scream.

Gluskap had never heard such a terrible racket. He covered his ears, danced his war dances, chanted the most fearful of spells, and sang songs that would have raised the dead, but Wasis paid no attention.

Unrelentingly, the baby went on. "Wahh! Wahh! Wahh!" He emitted a hellish shriek more powerful than any thunder or storm. The invincible Gluskap could not stand it anymore and ran away. He was so afraid of meeting the terrible Wasis again that he never went back to that village.

OYOTE WAS taking a walk with his friend Rabbit. Winter had recently ended, and the two were enjoying the warm spring sun. Coyote was still wearing his heavy winter blanket. As the day was so hot, he wanted to get rid of it. When he saw a large round rock, he thought he would take advantage of the current situation to show how generous he was.

He took off the blanket and threw it on the rock. "Here is something to protect you from the cold, friend rock," he said.

Rabbit was astonished by the gesture. "This is a magic rock. What you give her you cannot take back," he warned.

Coyote did not listen and left the blanket on the rock. A short while later a freezing wind blew down from the mountains. Clouds blocked the sun. Rain and hail beat the earth. Coyote and Rabbit ran into a cave, and soon Coyote began to feel cold. He thought of the blanket he had so carelessly given the rock and decided to retrieve it. Coyote returned to the rock and tore off the blanket. "What use do you have for a blanket?" he said. "You have been here for eternity and never needed one. Now I need it."

When Coyote turned to go, he heard a great racket behind him. The rock was determined to take the blanket back, and had started rolling after him. Coyote ran to the cave. "Run, Rabbit! There is a rock that wants to make little rugs out of us!"

The rock tumbled toward them in a most menacing way. Rabbit climbed up a hill, while Coyote took refuge in the forest, but the rock did not stop. It knocked over gigantic trees as if they were straw. It crossed rivers and prairies, chasing poor Coyote, who was running as fast as he could. Coyote called to the other animals for help. A herd of buffalo stampeded over to help Coyote, but they were all knocked over. The bears tried to help as well, but they were also stopped. Coyote was about to give up when a little bird flew to him. "I will help you, Coyote," he said. "Let the rock run over me."

Coyote moved aside and the rock rolled over the little bird who immediately shouted, "Cheep! Cheep!" The rock burst into many pieces that scattered in every direction and formed what we know today as the Rocky Mountains. Coyote escaped, and he never gave his blanket to a rock again!

TA-REN-YA-WA-GON, Upholder of the Heavens, was sleeping peacefully on his quilted pad above the clouds when he heard desperate shouts and moans coming from below. He looked down and saw the men and women of Earth being pursued by horrible monsters, cruel giants, and other fierce beasts.

The Sky Being felt compassion for the people and went to help them. Taking on the appearance of a human and thus becoming mortal, he joined the frightened people. He took a little girl by the hand. "Have no fear and follow me," he said.

He led the people in the direction of the rising sun until they arrived in a place where two great rivers met and created a roaring waterfall. Fertile plains extended in every direction, and Ta-ren-ya-wa-gon decided that

it was the perfect place to settle his people.

Many years passed, and many children were born. The people were happy, and Ta-ren-ya-wa-gon lived among them as an ordinary mortal. But before long there were too many people for this one place so the Sky Being called everyone together. "The time has come to look for a new land," he said. "Come with me and great nations will be born from you."

Ta-ren-ya-wa-gon took a little girl by the hand and the people followed him as they had before. When they came to a river,

the Sky Being turned to one of the families who followed him. "You are the Mohawk tribe," he declared. "This will be your land."

As soon as he gave them the new name, the Mohawks began to speak a new language. He gave them corn and beans to sow. He gave them dogs to help them hunt. This is why the Mohawks became so skilled at getting food.

The Sky Being took another little girl by the hand and led the others westward. After a long journey they came to a beautiful

valley surrounded by streams and forests. The Sky Being ordered another group to remain there. He named them Oneida, and in that very moment their language changed from that of the others. The Sky Being taught the Oneida many things, and this is why they became so wise.

Ta-ren-ya-wa-gon continued west with the rest of the people until he came to the base of a great mountain. He separated yet another group of families. "This is Onondaga Mountain, and you will be the nation that bears that name," he said.

The Onondaga also received their own language. Acquiring the mountain's strength, they became great warriors.

The Sky Being continued his journey as he led another little girl by the hand. When he arrived on the shores of a lake, he again chose a group of families. "You will be the Cayuga nation," he said.

He changed their language and taught them how to use canoes. The Cayuga thus became skilled at maneuvering their boats even in the most turbulent waters.

Taking another girl's hand, Ta-ren-ya-wa-gon led the last group of people to a region rich in mountains and lakes. "You will be the Seneca, and because you have traveled more than any of the others, your feet will be the swiftest," he declared.

After establishing the Five Nations, Ta-ren-ya-wa-gon decided to settle among the Onondaga and take the name of Hiawatha. He married a beautiful young woman with whom he had a daughter. The Five Nations prospered under Hiawatha's guidance.

One day foreigners came and threatened the people of the Five Nations. Hiawatha called the chiefs of each tribe he had created to come together. Accompanied by his daughter, he came to the meeting in a white canoe that floated in the sky. As soon as he landed, however, a terrifying bird

larger than ten eagles appeared. Hiawatha's daughter recognized it as the Great Bird of Mystery. She climbed onto its wings and, after bidding her father farewell, disappeared into the clouds. Hiawatha suffered greatly at the loss of his daughter, but after three days' silence, he spoke to the tribal chiefs as he had first intended. "You must be like the five fingers of a hand," he said. "If you are tight like a fist you will defeat all enemies!"

And so the powerful League of the Five Nations, also known as the Native American tribe the Iroquois, was born. Hiawatha climbed aboard his white canoe and, to the sounds of birdsong, disappeared forever into the sky.

MANY YEARS AGO the Cherokee people lived in a world so dark that they constantly bumped into one another and were forced to grope their way around. "We cannot go on like this," the people grumbled. "We need light!"

Fox told them of a people he knew who lived on the other side of the world with lots of light that they kept for themselves. He said they would not give up even a little bit of it. Opossum offered to go there and steal a piece. "I have a long, bushy tail, and it would be easy for me to hide the light in it," he said.

And so Opossum journeyed to the other side of the world. There he saw that a great Sun shone. Very slowly, he crawled up to the Sun, took a little light, and hid it in his tail. But the light was so hot that it immediately burned off his fur. Opossum could not help but yell out loud and his theft was

discovered. Forced to return the light, Opossum was escorted from that part of the world and returned home with a tail that has been hairless ever since.

When Eagle saw Opossum's failure, he decided to give it a try. "I will try," he said. "I will put the light on my head and bring it to you."

When Eagle arrived on the other side of the world, he flew up to the Sun, grabbed a ray, and placed it on his head, but it was so hot that it immediately burned his feathers. Eagle yelled in pain. The people of that part of the world scolded him and made him replace the ray of Sun. Like Opossum, Eagle returned to the Cherokee people without light and has been bald ever since. Witnessing his defeat, Grandmother Spider decided she would go. "Let me try!" she said.

Before she left, Grandmother Spider made a very strong clay pot and spun a thread long enough to reach the other side of the world. Only then did she begin her journey. Grandmother Spider was very small and so no one noticed her on her way to the Sun. She took a piece of it and swiftly placed it in the pot. She was quick, so the sun did not burn her and no one noticed. Grandmother Spider climbed the thread she had created and headed home.

And that was how Grandmother Spider brought Sun to the Cherokee. She also taught them to light a fire and to make clay pots like the one she had used to capture the sun. The Cherokee were forever grateful.

IN A LODGE AT THE foot of a mountain lived three Navaho brothers. The two eldest were skilled hunters while the youngest spent his time wandering around the canyons talking to plants and animals. He was not considered very bright. In the evening, when his older brothers came back from hunting, he would tell them all about the fantastic stories he had heard during the day. His brothers would get annoyed as they listened to the tales and would demand that he make himself useful instead of always wasting time and pretending he could understand the language of the plants and animals.

There soon came a time when the game the older brothers hunted became scarce, and so they were forced to travel farther and farther away for their food. One day the men did not return. On the sixth day of their absence, the younger brother decided to go look for them.

He walked for many hours. When evening fell he took shelter in a cave near a canyon. As he settled inside, he heard a great rustling of wings outside. He went to the cave's opening and saw a large number of

crows flapping about the canyon. Some crows perched on a nearby tree branch and began talking among themselves.

"Have you heard?" one of them said. "Two of us were killed by hunters."

"Everyone is talking about it. How did it happen?" asked one of the others.

"Our friends saw two hunters kill twelve deer at the bottom of the canyon," a third crow explained. "They hoped to steal a bit of meat, but the hunters killed them with their arrows before they had a chance."

The young man quickly realized that the hunters the crows were speaking about were his brothers. He lay down and soon fell asleep. Toward morning, an enchanting song filled the air. The young man was sure it was Hasjelti, the Dawn-Bringer, singing. Hasjelti, one of the Divine People, was famous for his beautiful songs. As the sun rose above the horizon, the song ceased, and the crows flew away. The young man set out to look for his brothers.

He found them at the bottom of a canyon and immediately told them what he had heard. The brothers were sure he was telling another one of his stories, but their brother knew exactly how many deer and how many crows they had killed. Could it be that a

man could understand the language of crows?

The three brothers decided to go back to their lodge. When they were halfway home they saw four wild goats climbing among the rocks. "You are more rested than we are," the eldest brothers said to the youngest. "Take the bow and these arrows and kill us a goat."

The young man hid behind a bush and waited until the goats were close enough. When they were in shooting range, he took an arrow and prepared to draw the bow, but his arm became paralyzed. As the goats walked by, he again tried to shoot them, but it was as if his arm were dead.

When the goats reached a plateau they suddenly transformed, taking on the appearance of Divine Ones. One was Hasjelti, the Dawn-Bringer; another was his brother, Hostjoghon, the Dusk-Bringer; the third was the hunchbacked Naaskiddi, the Seed-Bringer; and the fourth was Hastsezini, the Fire-Bringer. The young man fainted with fright as he witnessed the transformation. The four Divine Ones made a circle around him, traced symbols in the sand, and played their lutes until he awoke. "Why did you try to kill us?" they said. "Do you not know that you are one of us?"

The youth looked down and saw that he had become a wild sheep!

"Do not be afraid," Hasjelti said to him. "Come with us and I will teach you to dance."

In the meantime, the young man's brothers had gone looking for him. They searched everywhere and finally resigned themselves to returning to the lodge without him. The Divine Ones were invisible to their eyes, and they could not see what had happened to their brother either.

The youth was taken to the place of the Divine People. They were all very beautiful, but the most beautiful was surely Hasjelti. In the evening the fires were lit. The Dawn-Bringer taught the boy all the steps of the sacred dances. Throughout the night he explained the way to dress, the masks to wear, and the songs to sing. In the morning he gave him two ears of corn and said good-bye. The young man closed his eyes and a second later found himself all alone on the plateau.

The young man returned home and told his brothers everything he had been through. Because of his knowledge, the brothers were finally forced to believe his stories. The boy eventually taught the Navaho everything he had learned from the Divine People. And still today, after so many years, the Navahos perform Hasjelti's dance just as the young man first learned it.

QUETZALCOATL, who was shaped like a serpent, ruled the City of the Gods. He was good and generous, knowing neither arrogance nor hatred. All the other gods and goddesses loved him except his brother Tezcatlipoca, the god of night and lightning, who could not bear his goodness.

One day, Tezcatlipoca—also called Smoking Mirror because of a mirror he had that allowed him to see the thoughts of others —played a trick on his brother. He gathered friends together and, as Quetzalcoatl slept, used his magic to turn his brother into a man. When Quetzalcoatl awoke,

Tezcatlipoca placed his mirror before him. "Look what you have become!" he declared.

As soon as Quetzalcoatl saw his new face, he realized that all human needs and desires had entered him. "I cannot show myself to my people this way!" he exclaimed. "Shame has descended upon me, and now I am no longer worthy to be the ruler of the City of the Gods."

Quetzalcoatl summoned his twin brother, Xolotl the coyote, and entreated him to create a mask that could remind Quetzalcoatl of what he once looked like. The coyote made Quetzalcoatl a cape of green, red, and white feathers,

as well as a turquoise-colored mask in the shape of a serpent. This is why Quetzalcoatl took the name Plumed Serpent.

Although he had managed to change his brother, the evil Tezcatlipoca was not yet satisfied. He wanted his brother dead but did not dare kill him, lest the gods and goddesses who were friends with Quetzalcoatl avenge him. So Tezcatlipoca made a potion. He prepared a cup of pulque, a liquor made from the agave plant, and offered it to his brother. "Drink this medicine," he told his brother. "It will turn you back to what you were before."

Quetzalcoatl drank the liquor. He quickly became drunk, and Tezcatlipoca took advantage of his state to urge him to commit evil acts. When Quetzalcoatl was himself again, he realized the disgraceful things he had done and was so ashamed that he decided to kill himself.

Quetzalcoatl ordered his servants to build a great stone box. When it was finished, he lay down in it and remained there for four days without food or water. At the end of the fourth day, he called his servants. "Bring all my treasures here and lock them in the box," he commanded.

The servants obeyed. When the box was filled to the brim, they closed it and sealed it so that no one would ever be able to open it. Quetzalcoatl went to the seashore, put on his feather cape and his mask, and set himself on fire. From his ashes the majestic quetzal birds rose

with their long tails and green, red, and white feathers. As the birds circled in the sky, Quetzalcoatl's spirit and his brother Xolotl descended to the Land of the Dead, the home of Mictlantecuhtli, father of the gods and goddesses and guardian of the Precious Bones.

Xolotl and Quetzalcoatl's spirit asked for some of the precious bones, but Mictlantecuhtli refused. "It is dangerous," explained the god as he pointed to a little pile. "These bones belonged to creatures whom the gods killed because of their wickedness. It would be a disaster if they came back to life."

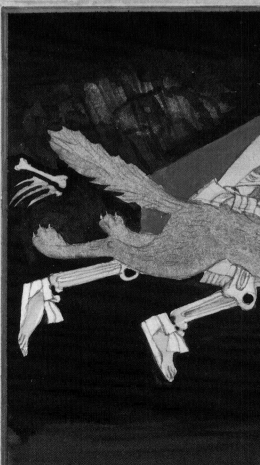

Xolotl the coyote realized the father god would never give up the bones, and so, quick as lightning, he grabbed one in his teeth and ran. Quetzalcoatl raced after him, as Mictlantecuhtli shouted, "Give me back that bone! What you want to do is too dangerous!"

The bone slipped out of Xolotl's mouth and broke into two pieces, one large and one small. As Quetzalcoatl picked up the pieces and ran toward the opening that led out of the Land of the Dead, he cut his finger on the jagged edge of the bone. When he emerged, he stopped and let a few drops of his blood fall onto the two

bones. Xolotl added his own magic, and a few days later two children were born from the bones, one boy and one girl. They were the first people of the new race of human beings.

Quetzalcoatl taught them to grow corn, make bowls, weave cloth, create mosaics,

and polish jade. He also taught them how to study the stars and calculate the days of the year. When he finished his lessons he boarded a raft of serpents and went out to sea. But before he was out of sight, Quetzalcoatl promised that he would someday return.

QUETZALCOATL had given human beings their life, but now he had to find a food that was right for them to eat. He looked at the flowers, fruits, and roots of many plants, but nothing seemed right. Then he noticed a red ant dragging a kernel of corn.

"This is the right food for human beings," thought Quetzalcoatl. "Little sister, where did you find this marvelous food?" he said to the ant. "The people to whom I have given life need it."

"I do not care about your people!" the ant retorted. "You go your way, and I will go mine."

"You presumptuous little thing," Quetzalcoatl replied. "If you do not tell me right now where these kernels come from I will eat you."

The red ant took the god to Tonacatepetl, otherwise known as Food Mountain. When they arrived she quickly slipped into a crack, confident that Quetzalcoatl could not follow her. But he turned himself into a black ant and chased after her. He followed her through countless long and winding tunnels until he came to a large cavern filled with kernels of corn. He had finally found the food, but how would he get it to his people? He went to ask the elder gods and goddesses for advice. "Only Nanahuatzin and the four Tlalocs can split Food Mountain and take the seeds," they said.

Quetzalcoatl turned to the god Nanahuatzin, who immediately summoned the gods of rain and thunder, and the blue, white, yellow, and red Tlalocs. Then Nanahuatzin and his friends went to Food Mountain. They sang magic chants and performed secret dances until their powers

came together and the mountain fell open. Kernels of white, black, yellow, and red corn poured out of the mountain along with a great quantity of peas, beans, and other edible seeds.

The Tlalocs took the seeds to the human beings, and Quetzalcoatl taught them how to grow corn so they would never be hungry again. Since that time corn has been considered the greatest of the divine gifts, and, still today, the Tlalocs are honored as the protectors of the harvest.

XQUIC, A WOMAN who had escaped the Realm of the Dead, had two twin sons, Hunahpu and Xbalanque, both of whom loved to play ball. Xquic did not want her sons to play the game because she feared that what had happened to their father would also happen to them. When her sons refused to listen to her pleas and threats, she decided to tell them the story of their father, Hun.

Hun had had a twin brother named Vucub. Both of them were such skilled players that the Lords of Death challenged them to a game of ball. Led by four owls, Hun and Vucub were led into the subterranean realm of Xibalba and were accompanied into a great hall. What appeared to be many people waiting for them, were in reality only mannequins. The twins did not realize this and thought they were real. They bowed before two statues. "Greetings to you, Lords of Death," they said.

The real Lords of Death, who had taken their places among the mannequins, revealed themselves and laughed. "Ha ha! You are the great ball players? So great that you pay your respects to wooden statues?"

Hun and Vucub angrily demanded that the match begin immediately. They did not like to be ridiculed. The Lords of Death took them to the playing field and invited them to sit on a stone bench that had secretly been heated. Hun and Vucub unsuspectingly sat down, and immediately leapt up, howling with pain. They jumped and ran about the field amid the whistles and laughter of the spectators. The ball game had to be put off to the following day.

The Lords of Death then led Hun and Vucub to the room where they were to spend the

night. They handed the brothers flaming torches. "Make sure these torches stay lit," they warned them. "If you let them go out, you will die."

Hun and Vucub watched the torches carefully, but they were made only of reeds. There was nothing the twins could do and in no time the torches burned to ashes. In the morning, Hun and Vucub were put to death.

That was the story that Xquic told her sons, Hunahpu and Xbalanque. But even the story of their father's death did not dissuade them. The two young sons continued to play their favorite game until they became the best players in the region.

One day four owls came to them. "We are the messengers of the Lords of Death. Our rulers wish to challenge you to the ball game," they said.

Like Hun and Vucub, Hunahpu and Xbalanque were taken to Xibalba. But because they knew the story of their father and uncle, they were ready for the practical jokes of the Lords of Death. As they expected, the Lords took them into the room filled with statues. The twins were unable to pick out the Lords of the Death among the mannequins so they sent Xan the mosquito to bite their legs. The Lords of Death cried out and started to scratch. "Greetings to you, Lords of Death!" the twins said in response.

The Lords of Death then tried to get them to sit on the burning hot bench, but Hunahpu and Xbalanque claimed that they preferred to sit on the ground. When the Lords of Death gave them the torches, the twins withdrew to their room and immediately put out the flames and replaced them with red feathers. The Lords checked on them through a peephole throughout the night. Fooled by the red feathers, they thought the torches were lit and could not understand why they did not burn up. In the morning,

the twins appeared with the torches completely intact.

So the Lords of Death were forced to play ball against the twins. They were extremely ashamed when they were soundly beaten in front of all the people of Xibalba. Consequently, they would not give up until they had killed the twins. The twins possessed magic that would return them to life if they were ever killed, so they allowed the Lords to capture and burn them and to scatter their ashes in the sea. After doing so, the Lords of Death of course thought the twins were dead and went home happily.

Some time after they had resurrected themselves, Hunahpu and Xbalanque wandered through Xibalba once more, disguised as beggars and performing all kinds of spells. One day they appeared before the Lords of Death. As the Lords watched, the twins killed a dog and then brought it back to life. The rulers, delighted by the miracle, wished the beggars to perform the trick on them, as well. They prepared a burning pyre and threw themselves upon it.

As soon as they did so, the twins threw off their disguises. They revealed their true identity and declared that they had come to avenge their father. Naturally, they did not return the Lords of Death to life.

VIRACOCHA, THE Creator god, had four sons and four daughters whom he sent into the mortal world to create an empire. The first son, Cachi, was so mischievous that his brothers closed him up in a cave and never let him out again. The second, Ucho, turned himself into a stone idol so that he could be forever worshiped. The third, Sauco, decided to remain with the peasants and help them with their crops. The fourth, Manco, went on with his sisters until he arrived at a clearing. He stuck a golden stick into the ground. "This is where we will stop," he said. "In this place I will create the capital of my empire."

Manco went to work but soon realized that it was very difficult to build houses in that clearing. A strong wind blew day and night, so strong that it even knocked over huge boulders. Manco decided to imprison the wind in a llama pen.

Later that day, Manco's brother Sauco came to him. "I am the wind's friend, and I have not seen him in my part of the country," he said. "Do you know what happened to him?"

Manco explained to his brother what he had done.

"You may keep the wind prisoner, but only today. At sunset you have to set him free," Sauco replied.

That meant that Manco had only one day to build his city. How would it be possible?

Manco braided a very long, strong rope, climbed to the top of the highest mountain, and waited for the sun to pass overhead. As soon as it did, Manco threw the rope and lassoed it, then swiftly tied the other end of the rope to the mountain peak. The sun

tried to free itself by burning the rope with its blazing rays, but the rope was just too strong.

Weeks and months passed without the sun ever setting, and therefore it seemed that the day never ended. This was how Manco was able to build his capital and surround it with mountains. Only when he was finished did he free the sun. He freed the wind, too, which by now, kept at bay by the ring of mountains, could not do much damage. That was how Manco created the Incan Empire.

ONE NIGHT A long time ago, the creator god Kon-Tiki Viracocha created a group of giants. They were beings that had extraordinary strength and were able to lift mountains and divert rivers. They soon became so proud of their strength that they became arrogant, defying even Kon-Tiki himself. The giants rebelled and tried to exile Kon-Tiki, but the god, in anger, turned them all into stone statues. With his favored companions, he withdrew into Lake Titicaca.

For many years the Earth remained dark and desolate. One day Kon-Tiki came out of the lake with his companions. "For too long this place has been sad and solitary," he said. "I want life to thrive here once again."

First he created the sun and the moon, so that day and night would each have their proper light. Then he filled every place with plants and animals. When he was done with that he took rocks and began to sculpt them into human shape. Every statue was sculpted and dressed according to what it would become. Kon-Tiki created a variety of people including a chief, a

soldier, a peasant, a princess, a weaver, a cook, a little boy, and a little girl. When he had sculpted a sufficient number of statues, Kon-Tiki turned to his companions. "Now I will speak the name of each statue," he said. "You will carry the statues to the springs, caves, woods, and other places I direct you."

Kon-Tiki gave each statue its name, and the companions took them throughout the land to the places the god had chosen for each. When all the statues were in place, Kon-Tiki shouted, "Come out!" In that moment, men, women, and children were transformed from cold stone and started to move like human beings.

Kon-Tiki looked at his creatures and smiled with satisfaction. He had done a very good job indeed. The god set out on a journey to the north with his companions. In every place he stopped, the people he had created lit fires and erected sanctuaries. But one day, Kon-Tiki Viracocha disappeared. Ever since, many believe that he returned to his home beneath the waters of Lake Titicaca.

I N THE FOREST LIVED two giant monkeys who terrorized the people. No one had ever seen such huge, evil creatures. They invaded villages, stole food, destroyed homes, and attacked anyone who went into the forest alone. The monkeys were a constant menace, but fearing their strength and cunning, no one dared to hunt them.

In one of the many villages along the Amazon River lived three brothers of the Karaya tribe. The two eldest were skilled and courageous hunters, while the youngest, weak and delicate because of his ill health, had never learned to hunt. The older brothers one day decided that they had had enough of the evil creatures. "It is time to put a stop to those wicked monkeys," they declared to their younger brother. "You take care of the house while we go out and look for them."

The two brothers left and made their way into the thick of the forest, which was so dark that even the sun's light could not penetrate. They walked until they came to a pool of clear water. Tired and thirsty, they bent over to drink. All at once the water changed color and began to whirl about. Out of the water's swirl came a toad-woman so ugly that she made the brothers' flesh crawl.

The toad-woman approached the two hunters. "I know you are

looking for the monkeys' den," she said. "I will tell you where it is, and I will also tell you how you can fight them, but in return one of you must marry me."

The brothers were disgusted at such a suggestion. "Marry you? We would not think of it! Go on, get out of here, or we will thrash you," they replied.

The toad-woman withdrew into the waters from which she had come, and the hunters resumed their search. Suddenly

they heard savage screams coming from the leafy canopy above them. Two enormous monkeys dropped down like devils. Armed with long poles, the monkeys threw themselves at the hunters. Within minutes they had beaten them so badly that the two brothers were forced to flee into the deepest part of the forest.

Meanwhile, the youngest brother was trying to catch a bird near the house in order to have something to eat. His aim

was not very good, and he completely missed the bird when he shot his arrow. The bird flew away and the disappointed boy was left to search for his arrow. He looked right and left and up and down, but it seemed to have disappeared completely. He was about to give up when a snake peeped up from a hole. "My boy, your arrow has fallen into my hole," it said. "I will get it for you."

The snake retrieved the arrow and gave it to the young man. As he handed it to him, he noticed how frail and sick the boy was. The snake decided to give him a miraculous ointment that in an instant cured all his problems. The young man thanked the snake. "Now that I am well, I want to go in search of my brothers," he said.

"Be careful," the snake warned him as he handed him an arrow. "The monkeys that they are hunting are demons in disguise. Only with this magic arrow will you be able to defeat them. Also, on your way you will meet a toad-woman who will ask you to marry her. Accept. You will not be sorry."

The young man said good-bye to the snake and made his way into the forest with the magic arrow in hand, following the same path that his brothers had taken before him.

Eventually he came to the pool of water and met the toad-woman. As expected, she asked

him to marry her and the young man consented. The toad-woman led him to a big, dead tree. Inside was the monkeys' den.

"In a little while the monkeys will come out to drink," she said. "When you shoot your arrow you must aim between the eyes. You only have to hit one of the demons for the other to be defeated as well."

The young man settled down to wait and soon saw the monkeys come out of the hollow tree trunk. He aimed at the first one and pulled his bow back. His aim was off, but the arrow was magical and directed itself at the target. The arrow hit one of the monkeys and, as promised, both he and his fellow demon screamed and then disappeared, leaving only two monkey-skins on the ground.

The young man found his brothers and they returned to the village. He married the toad-woman, but, as the snake had said, he had nothing to regret. As soon as the toad-woman crossed the threshold of their new home, she turned into a beautiful maiden. In turn, the young man became a great hunter and lived a long, happy, and healthy life with his ravishing wife.

THERE ONCE LIVED a man named Bamapama whom everyone considered a little crazy, a bit of a thief, and definitely a lazy oaf. He and his people lived underground in a place where the sun never set but stayed in the same place in the sky. Life down there was rather monotonous, so Bamapama spent most of his time trying to find ways to entertain himself and get into mischief.

One day Bamapama, after some prank or another, was forced to leave the village in a hurry and stay away for a while. He decided to go to the surface of the earth to hunt. Many frightening legends were told about the world above, so much so that no one had ever been there. But Bamapama was a little crazy, and the tales did not scare him at all. He took his spear, traveled through a long passage, and came out on the earth's surface.

Once there, Bamapama saw a kangaroo hop by and immediately took off in pursuit. He had almost caught up with the animal when

the sun went down behind the horizon and it became dark. Bamapama had never seen nighttime and became very afraid. He climbed into a tree to try to get out of the dark. Realizing he could not escape it and overcome by exhaustion, he came down and fell asleep.

In the morning Bamapama was astonished to see the sun again. "How wonderful!" he exclaimed. "Here you run during the day and sleep at night."

Bamapama went back to his people to tell them what had happened. At first no one believed him, because Bamapama, besides being a little crazy, was also known to bend the truth. But he was so persistent in his story that his friends finally agreed to go and see for themselves.

Bamapama took everyone up to the earth's surface. When it turned dark, the people, filled with fear, fled up into the trees.

"Do not be afraid," Bamapama said. "You will see tomorrow morning that the sun will be back."

In the morning the sun did indeed come up and everyone looked around in wonder. "Bamapama may be a little crazy, but he is also very clever!" they exclaimed.

And they stayed on the earth's surface from that day forward.

M AUI WAS A BORN trickster who loved to fool people with a thousand pranks. It was therefore easy to understand why his brothers did not show much enthusiasm when they had to take Maui fishing with them.

"He is sure to make all kinds of trouble," they said.

Their bad mood became even worse when Maui insisted on taking the boat so far out into the open sea that they could no longer see the land. He claimed there would be good fishing there, so his brothers complied and dropped their nets into the water. But after many hours they did not catch even the tiniest of fish. They were also so tired that they could not keep their eyes open.

"Sleep peacefully," Maui said. "I will take care of the fishing."

The brothers laughed. Maui had never fished in his life, and they could not imagine how he was going to catch something when they had gotten nothing. Nevertheless, they agreed to let him fish and lay down in the bottom of the boat to rest. While his brothers slept, Maui cast his fishing line in the water and sang:

Maui of a thousand ruses,
He does whatever he chooses!
Maui of a thousand schemes,
A better fisherman was never seen!

When his brothers awoke, they saw Maui struggling to reel in something big and heavy. When

they peered through the water they saw a strange green and brown shape that could have been anything except a fish.

"What kind of animal could that be?" his brothers wondered. "Maui probably caught the hull of an old boat."

As Maui continued to haul in the fishing line, it became clear that the object was much bigger than a boat.

"Let it go," his brothers told him.

But Maui certainly had no intention of letting his first catch get away. With one hand over the other, Maui huffed and yanked, and succeeded at last. As the object was brought to the water's surface, everyone gasped in shock when they saw what Maui had caught.

"It is an island!" his brothers exclaimed. "Incredible! Maui caught a whole island!"

"Not bad for a beginner, is it?" Maui asked, smirking.

That was the first island of Polynesia brought from the bottom of the sea. Maui eventually fished up each of the Polynesian islands. Although he became a great hero, he never gave up being the greatest trickster in Polynesia!

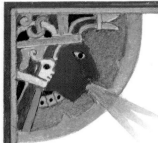

* EUROPE *

ALBA LONGA. The ancient Italian city of Latium that was founded by Ascanius, son of Aeneas, a Trojan hero. The last kings who conquered Alba Longa before Rome was built were Procas, Amulius, and Numitor. The city was destroyed by the Roman king Tullus Hostilius.

ARTHUR. The legendary king of the Britons who was raised by Merlin the magician. After Arthur drew the magic sword Excalibur from the stone, he became king and founded the Round Table, a gathering of knights dedicated to the search for the Holy Grail, the chalice from which Jesus drank at the Last Supper. Arthur left his world for the magic island of Avalon on a ship guided by three fairy queens.

DAEDALUS. The Greek sculptor and architect from Athens who was said to sculpt statues that moved their eyes and arms. He was forced to flee Athens after killing his nephew Talos. With his son Icarus, Daedalus built the Labyrinth in Crete at the command of King Minos as a home for the king's son the Minotaur. After the Minotaur was killed, Daedalus escaped the Labyrinth and

King Arthur

Crete with the wings he built and went to Italy to take refuge with Cocalus, king of Sicily.

HADES. The Greek god of the Underworld. Hades is also used to describe the name of the Underworld itself. The Underworld is composed of Erebus, the section to which the dead go as soon as they die, and Tartarus, the deepest region, home of the souls of the wicked.

Heracles

HERACLES. The most popular demigod in Greece, also known as Hercules. He performed twelve famous labors, which included fighting the invulnerable lion of Nemea; killing the Hydra of Lerna, a nine-headed serpent; capturing the fierce boar of Mount Erymanthus; bringing back alive the sacred stag of Cerynitia; driving away the Stymphalian birds whose wings and beaks were made of bronze; taking Hippolyta's girdle; cleaning Augeas's vast stables; bringing back a savage bull from Crete; capturing Diomedes' mares, which ate human-flesh; bringing back the cattle of Geryon, a three-bodied monster; bringing back the golden apples of the Hesperides; and capturing the dog Cerberus.

Opposite: Niflheim

HESPERIDES. The three Greek nymphs who live in a beautiful garden enclosed within high walls and protect the golden apples of Hera's tree. They are helped by a hundred-headed dragon, Ladon.

KASCHEI. In Russian legends this mythical evil magician could not be killed because his soul did not dwell in his body, but in an egg hidden among the roots of a tree (or inside a duck or a rabbit). Prince Ivan discovered this secret hiding place and was able to kill him.

MARS. The Roman god of war, identified with the Greek god Ares. Mars is also the father of Romulus, who is said to have founded Rome.

MEDUSA. The Greek maiden whom Athena transformed into a monster because she boasted about her beauty. Medusa has flames for eyes, snakes instead of hair, enormous fangs, and the power to turn anyone who looks at her into stone.

Medusa

Odin

Paris and Helen

Romulus

NIFLHEIM. In Nordic myth, it is the world of ice and mist and the lowest region of the underworld and is ruled by Hel, the goddess of the Underworld. Other Nordic mythological places include Muspelheim, the land of fire; Asgard, the home of the gods; and Valhalla, the region of Asgard inhabited by the heroes who die in battle and by the Valkyries, woman warriors, including Brunhild, whose task it is to guide the heroes in the battles of the sky.

ODIN. The Lord of the Viking gods who is known as Woden by the Germanic peoples. He is the god of wisdom who belongs to the race of the Aesir, along with Frigga, Odin's wife; Thor, the god of thunder; and Balder, the son of Odin and Frigga. Odin also governs Loki, the troublemaker; Freya, the goddess of love; and her son Frey, the god of fertility. Odin has only one eye, rides an eight-legged horse, and is always accompanied by two crows called "thought," and "memory."

OLYMPUS. The Greek mountain where Zeus lives with his wife, Hera, and his children, other gods and goddesses: Athena, the goddess of wisdom; Aphrodite, the goddess of love; Ares, the god of war; Hermes (Maia, not Hera, was Hermes' mother), the messenger of the gods and protector of travelers; and Apollo, the god of beauty and music. Hephaestus, the god of fire, was exiled from Olympus because he was so ugly. He then went to live in Italy, inside Mount Etna, a volcano. Artemis, the goddess of the hunt, left Olympus because she preferred to live in the woods.

PARIS. The prince of Troy whose father, Priam, abandoned him because of a dream he had that Paris would one day destroy his country. The dream came true with Paris's abduction of Helen, the wife of Menelaus. Aphrodite promised Helen to Paris as a gift for judging her the most beautiful of all the goddesses. His abduction of Helen caused a war between the Greeks and Trojans that lasted ten years and ended with a Greek victory and the death of Paris.

ROMULUS AND REMUS. The twin sons of Rhea Silvia and the god Mars, and nephews of Numitor, the king of Alba Longa. They were first raised by a wolf and then by Faustulus, a shepherd. Romulus killed his brother Remus and founded Rome.

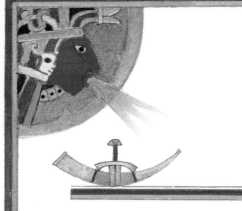

★ THE AMERICAS ★

SIEGFRIED. Also called Sigurd. The German hero and son of Woden, who killed Fafner, the last of the race of the giants, who had turned himself into a dragon in order to guard the magic ring of the Nibelungen. After he retrieved the ring, Siegfried married Brunhild. The dragon's blood had made Siegfried invulnerable except for one place on his shoulder where a linden leaf had fallen. Siegfried was eventually killed by a

Siegfried

spear thrown by his enemy Hagen that struck him in that exact spot.

THESEUS. The most famous Greek hero, who accomplished many seemingly impossible feats. With the help of Ariadne, the daughter of King Minos, he killed the Minotaur; he fought the Centaurs, half horses and half men; he descended into Erebus to abduct Persephone, wife of the god Hades, but was forced to sit in the Chair of Forgetfulness where his mind almost became blank, until he was freed by Heracles;

Theseus

with the help of the Argonauts he took the Golden Fleece.

ZEUS. The father and lord of the Greek gods and goddesses. His brothers are

Zeus

Hades, the god of the land of the dead, and Poseidon, the god of the sea. His wife is Hera, protector of married women. Zeus presides over atmospheric phenomena and, when he is angry at human beings, throws lightning bolts to Earth.

ALGONQUIANS. Native American people of North America who make up many tribes including the Arapaho, Cheyenne, Micmac, and Delaware. They lived across a wide geographical area that extended from the Atlantic Ocean to the Rocky Mountains. The tribes developed a complex mythology that varies from region to region. For example, Gluskap, an eastern Algonquian hero, can be called Michabo, Nanabozo, or Wisagatcak, and, depending upon the particular tribe, can be considered either good or evil.

Aztecs

AZTECS. An ancient Native American people who lived in the area of what is today Mexico. Their civilization collapsed in 1519 as a result of the Spanish conquest led by Hernando Cortez. Their chief god was Quetzalcoatl. Other important deities included Huitzilopochtli, the god of war, to whom the Aztecs sacrificed thousands of people every year, and the four Tlalocs, the gods of rain and harvests.

CHEROKEE. Native American people who were moved to a reservation in Oklahoma from their native lands in what are today parts of Tennessee, the Carolinas, Georgia, and Alabama. In their mythology, the Earth was once suspended from the Sky by four ropes that broke, thus dropping Earth into the Ocean.

COYOTE. To many Native Americans, Coyote (often portrayed as a coyote-man) is the "trickster," who wanders eternally and practices pranks and deceit.

CROW. The Inuit of Alaska believe that Crow, whom they call Tulugaukuk, created the world.

GLUSKAP. The principal hero of the eastern Algonquian Native Americans who is extremely strong and has the ability to turn into a giant. He is also an expert in the magic arts. Gluskap is good and he protects human beings from the evil beings that menace them.

Coyote

GRANDMOTHER SPIDER.
The Cherokee creator goddess. Spiders are female creators in the Hopi tradition as well.

HASJELTI. Navahos believe that they descend from a mysterious, subterranean people known as the People of Saints, in whose honor they perform ceremonies with songs and prayers. Hasjelti, the Dawn-Bringer, is one of the People of Saints. Among the others are

Inuit

Hostjoghon, the Dusk-Bringer; Naaskiddi, the Seed-Bringer; and Hastsezini, the Fire-Bringer.

HIAWATHA. The historical sixteenth-century figure who founded the powerful Iroquois alliance that was initially composed of five tribes (Mohawk, Oneida, Cayuga, Onondaga, and

Gluskap

Seneca) and later included one more (Tuscarora). Hiawatha became a legendary figure and is identified with Ta-ren-ya-wa-gon, the Celestial Divine Being.

HUNAHPU AND XBALANQUE. The twin heroes of Mayan mythology who represent the victory of human beings over evil divinities and death.

INCAS. The ancient Native American people of the Andes mountains. The Incas' empire extended over much of what is today known as Peru and Ecuador as well as parts of Bolivia, Chile, and Brazil. The Incan emperor was considered divine and a direct descendant of the Sun. The Incas usually sacrificed llamas to their god Viracocha, but sometimes performed human sacrifices as well.

Hunahpu and Xbalanque

INUIT. A people who live in the cold regions of North America and survive almost exclusively by hunting and trading in pelts. Their mythology endows all natural things—animals, mountains, lakes, rocks, and stones—with a soul. The most powerful spirits are those of the air, the sea, and the moon.

IROQUOIS. The Native American people of allied tribes who occupied a vast area of North America from the Atlantic coast to Lake Ontario. The Iroquois alliance was originally made

up of five nations: Mohawk, Oneida, Cayuga, Onondaga, and Seneca. In 1715 they were joined by the Tuscarora.

KON-TIKI VIRACOCHA. A deity of the Collas, an Andean people who lived in the area of Lake Titicaca, between Peru and Bolivia. The name Viracocha, which originally identified an Incan god, was added to Kon-Tiki's after the Incas conquered the Collas.

Incas

MANCO. Also called Ayar Manco and Manco Capac, he is an Incan hero who founded cities and created civilization. Tradition credits him with teaching agriculture and the laws of social organization to the Incas.

MAYA. An Indian people who lived in parts of the Yucatan in Mexico and in parts of Guatemala. Mayan society before the Spanish conquest was highly evolved; the Maya made sculptures and paintings and built

Maya

great cities of stone. Scholars of the Mayans believe the Mayan supreme god was called Itzamna.

MICTLANTECUHTLI. The Aztec god of the Underworld and of death. He guards the bones of the dead in order to prevent anyone from pouring blood on them and thus bringing back to life the person to whom they belonged.

NAVAHO. The Native American people whose reservation extended through areas of New Mexico and Arizona in a region that was rich in coal and oil. Their mythology,

Mictlantecuhtli

ceremonies, and dances are very similar to those of their neighbors, the Pueblo Indians.

QUETZALCOATL. The most important Aztec deity, he is the god of the sky and the sun, the winds and the morning star. He is also known as the Plumed Serpent and is considered a great benefactor of the human race.

RABBIT. In many Native American tales, Rabbit is Coyote's friend and he often takes part in his adventures.

SIOUX. Native American people of the prairies who are divided into a number of tribes. The word means "little snakes." The Sioux worship Wakan Tanka, "the Great Mystery," the creator and ruler of the Universe.

Sioux

TEZCATLIPOCA. The Aztec god of the night and of witchcraft. He is an evil god who opposes his brother Quetzalcoatl with constant trickery.

VIRACOCHA. The Incan creator god whose legend subsequently merged with that of the Colla god Kon-Tiki. Nevertheless, distinct myths, such as the story of Manco and his Ayar brothers, survive.

XOLOTL. An Aztec god and Quetzalcoatl's twin, he is the lord of magic who is able to change forms. He often appears in the form of a coyote.

Xolotl

✳ ASIA ✳

AMATERASU. The beautiful Japanese goddess of the sun and of fertility who was born of Izanagi. According to one myth, the crops on Earth dried up when she hid in a cave from fear of her treacherous brother, Susanowo. Only when the

Amaterasu

other gods tricked her into coming out of the cave did vegetation come back to life.

AUGUST OF JADE. In Chinese, his name is Yu Huang. In the Taoist religion, the August of Jade is the supreme god, lord of the Sky and father of the gods and goddesses.

Izanagi and Izanami

IZANAGI AND IZANAMI. The myth of Izanagi and Izanami is the most important Japanese creation myth. Originally the two gods were joined together as one, but, in order to begin creation, they separated to create the Sky, Izanagi, and the Earth, Izanami. Izanagi later became the god of Life, and Izanami the goddess of Death. Izanagi is also believed to be the mother of Amaterasu, the beautiful goddess of the sun; Tsuki-Yomi, the god of the moon; and Susanowo,

Shepherd and Weaver

the violent and evil god of vengeance and thunder.

RAMA. The human incarnation of the Indian god Vishnu. He came down to Earth where he married beautiful Sita, daughter of King Janaka, and killed the bloodthirsty demon Ravana who had

captured Sita. Rama was assisted by his brother Lakshmana and by Sugriva, lord of the monkeys. Rama's exploits are recounted in the "Ramayana," an ancient Indian poem of almost one

hundred thousand verses that dates to the fourth century B.C.E.

RAVANA. The ten-headed, twenty-armed bandit-demon king of Lanka. The god Brahma granted Ravana the privilege of being invulnerable to any enemy, whether it be god or demon, but not to human beings, whom he considered too weak and insignificant to pose any threat. The story of Ravana is recounted in the Indian poem "Ramayana."

Ramayana

SHEPHERD AND WEAVER. These are the Chinese names for the constellations known in the European tradition as Lyra, the Lyre, and Aquila, the Eagle. "The Shepherd and the Weaver" is a popular myth that exists in many versions. After the August of Jade allowed the Shepherd and the Weaver to marry, he decreed that the two lovers could only meet on the seventh day of the seventh month. When it rains on that day in northern China, they say the rain is the tears of joy that the Shepherd and the Weaver are shedding at seeing one another.

TRIMURTI. The principal Indian divine triad that consists of Brahma, the creator of universes; Vishnu, who maintains and protects what Brahma has created; and Shiva, who destroys that which has come to the end of its existence.

Trimurti

VISHNU. One of the gods of the Trimurti, he is the protector of human beings and nature. According to Indian mythology, Vishnu came down to Earth ten separate times to save the world. His ten avatars, or "descents," occurred in various incarnations:
Matsya the Fish
Kurma the Turtle
Varaha the Boar
Narasinha the Lion-man
Vamana the Dwarf
Parashurama, a Man
Rama, a Prince
Krishna the Black Man
Buddha the Saint
Kalkin the Horse

Rama, King Janaka, and Sita

★ AFRICA & AUSTRALIA ★

Anubis

ANUBIS. The jackal-headed Egyptian god, son of Osiris and Nephthys, who is the lord of embalming and guardian of tombs. He leads the souls of the dead before Osiris, who judges them.

BAMAPAMA. A mythological figure of the Australian Aborigines who is also called Ure. Like the Native American Coyote, he is a trickster, a madman, and a transgressor of rules, but, unlike Coyote, Bamapama also uses his creativity for the benefit of human beings.

Bamapama

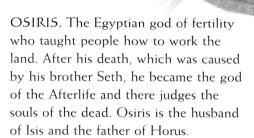

GEB. One of the nine great Egyptian deities, he was worshiped in the City of the Sun in Lower Egypt, as the god of Earth. Geb was the husband of Nut, goddess of the Heavenly Waters, and father of the four Divine Twins—Osiris, Isis, Seth, and Nephthys.

Geb

GULU. The Ugandan god of the sky and father of Nambi. Gulu rules the people and pastures of heaven and owns vast herds of cattle.

HORUS. The hawk-headed Egyptian god and lord of the sky who is the son of Isis and Osiris. He is also Seth's eternal enemy.

Horus and Isis

ISIS. The Egyptian mother-goddess, lady of love and destiny, who is the bride of Osiris and mother of Horus.

KINTU. A Ugandan king who is believed to have existed and been inserted into older myths so that his descendants might claim divine origins.

THE MANTIS. The "divine insect" of the Bosjesmans, the most ancient people of Africa. In their myths, the Creator God sometimes takes on the form of a praying mantis.

Maui

MAUI. A mythic hero of the Polynesians, also known as "Maui of the Thousand Tricks." He represents the clever hero who uses his craftiness to help the human race. Maui fished up the Polynesian islands, stole fire for his human beings, kept the sun in the sky without allowing it to set so that the day might have more light, and finally died in his attempt to obtain eternal life for his people.

NAMBI. The daughter of the Ugandan god Gulu, and wife of Kintu.

NEPHTHYS. The Egyptian goddess of death, and wife of Seth. She helped Isis find the body of Osiris, Isis's husband.

THE NILE RIVER. Egypt's sacred river, whose periodic flooding made the valley fertile.

NUT. The Egyptian goddess of the night sky and mother of the stars. Married to Geb, she gave birth to Osiris and his siblings.

OSIRIS. The Egyptian god of fertility who taught people how to work the land. After his death, which was caused by his brother Seth, he became the god of the Afterlife and there judges the souls of the dead. Osiris is the husband of Isis and the father of Horus.

Osiris

SETH. The Egyptian god of the desert, of storms, and of disorder. He is in never-ending conflict with Horus because he killed Horus's father Osiris, his brother.

SHU. The Egyptian god of air and of the light of the sun. He separated Geb and Nut, the Earth and the Sky, so that the world could be created.

Shu

FURTHER READING

Andersen, Johannes C. *Myths and Legends of the Polynesians.* New York: Dover Publications, 1995.

Arnott, Kathleen. *African Myths and Legends.* New York: Oxford University Press, 1990.

Barber, Richard, ed. *Arthurian Legends: An Illustrated Anthology.* Totowa: Littlefield Adams, 1979.

Bierhorst, John. *The Mythology of Mexico and Central America.* New York: Morrow, 1992.

Branston, Brian. *Gods of the North.* New York: Thames and Hudson, 1980.

Crossley-Holland, Kevin. *The Norse Myths.* New York: Pantheon, 1981.

Davis, F. Hadland. *Myths and Legends of Japan.* New York: Dover Publications, 1992.

Dixon-Kennedy, Mike. *Celtic Myth and Legend: An A–Z of People and Places.* New York: Sterling, 1998.

Erdoes, Richard and Alfonso Ortiz, eds. *American Indian Myths and Legends.* New York: Pantheon, 1985.

Gill, Sam D. and Irene F. Sullivan. *Dictionary of Native American Mythology.* New York: Oxford University Press, 1994.

Grant, Michael and John Hazel. *Who's Who in Classical Mythology.* New York: Oxford University Press, 1993.

Graves, Robert. *The Greek Myths.* New York: Penguin Books, 1993.

Hamilton, Edith. *Mythology.* New York: Penguin Books, 1989.

Mackenzie, Donald A. *Myths of China and Japan.* London: Gresham, N.D.

O'Flaherty, Wendy. *Hindu Myths: A Sourcebook.* New York: Viking Press, 1975.

Philip, Neil. *Myths and Legends.* New York: DK Publishing, Inc., 1999.

Philip, Neil. *Mythology.* New York: Alfred A. Knopf, 1999.

Radin, Paul A. *African Folktales.* New York: Schocken Books, 1983.

Rosenberg, Donna. *World Mythology: An Anthology of the Great Myths and Epics 2nd Edition.* Illinois: NTC Publishing Group, 1994.

Spence, Lewis. *The Myths of Mexico and Peru.* New York: Dover Publications, 1995.

———. *Ancient Egyptian Myths and Legends.* New York: Dover Publications, 1991.

Warner, Elizabeth. *Heroes, Monsters, and Other Worlds from Russian Mythology.* New York: Peter Bedrick Books, 1996

Werner, E.T.C. *Myths and Legends of China.* New York: Dover Publications, 1994.

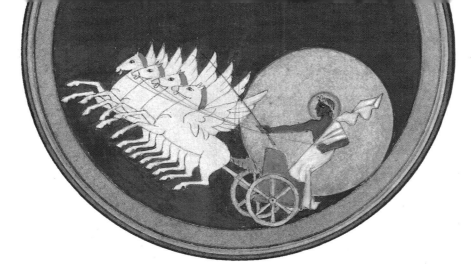

Editor, English-language edition
Lia Ronnen

Design Coordinator, English-language edition
Barbara Sturman

Translated from the Italian by
Alexandra Bonfante-Warren

Library of Congress Cataloging-in-Publication Data
Bini, Renata.
    [Miti e leggende di tutti i tempi. English]
    A world treasury of myths, legends, and folktales :
stories from six continents / as retold by Renata Bini ;
illustrations by Mikhail Fiodorov.
        p. cm.
    Summary: A collection of myths and legends from
many different cultures around the world, including
those of ancient Greece and the Great Plains Indians.
ISBN 0-8109-4554-1 (Abrams: cloth) / ISBN 0-8109-2720-9 (book club: pbk.)
    1. Mythology. 2. Legends. [1. Mythology.
2. Folklore.] I. Fiodorov, Mikhail, ill. II. Title.
BL311.B5613 2000
291.1'3—dc21   99–42602

Copyright © 1999 Happy Books, Milan
Published in 2000 by
Harry N. Abrams, Incorporated, New York

Printed and bound in Italy

 Harry N. Abrams, Inc.
100 Fifth Avenue
New York, N.Y. 10011
www.abramsbooks.com